"DOC." GORDON

MORE WILDSIDE CLASSICS

"DOC." GORDON

Mary E. Wilkins Freeman

WILDSIDE PRESS

"DOC." GORDON

This edition published 2005 by Wildside Press, LLC.
www.wildsidepress.com

CHAPTER I

It was very early in the morning, it was scarcely dawn, when the young man started upon a walk of twenty-five miles to reach Alton, where he was to be assistant to the one physician in the place, Doctor Thomas Gordon, or as he was familiarly called, "Doc." Gordon. The young man's name was James Elliot. He had just graduated, and this was to be his first experience in the practice of his profession of medicine. He was in his twenties. He was small, but from the springiness of his gait and the erectness of his head he gave an impression of height. He was very good-looking, with clearly-cut features, and dark eyes, in which shone, like black diamonds, sparks of mischief. They were honest eyes, too. The young fellow was still sowing his wild oats, but more with his hands than with his soul. He was walking because of a great amount of restless energy; he fairly revelled in stretching his legs over the country road in the keen morning air. The train service between Gresham, his home place, and Alton was very bad, necessitating two changes and waits of hours, and he had fretted at the prospect. When a young man is about to begin his career, he does not wish to sit hours in dingy little railroad stations on his way toward it. It was much easier, and pleasanter, to walk, almost run to it, as he was doing now. His only baggage was his little medicine-case; his trunk had gone by train the day before. He was very well dressed, his clothes had the cut of a city tailor. He was almost dandified. His father was well-to-do: a successful peach-grower on a wholesale scale. His great farm was sprayed over every spring with delicate rosy garlands of peach blossoms, and in the autumn the trees were heavy with the almond-scented fruit. He had made a fortune, and aside from that had achieved a certain local distinction. He was then mayor of Gresham, which had a city government. James was very proud of his father and fond of him. Indeed, he had reason to be. His father had done everything in his power for him, given him a good education, and supplied him liberally with money. James had always had a sense of plenty of money, which had kept him from undue love of it. He was now beginning the practice of his profession, in a small way, it is true, but that he recognized as expedient. "You had better get acclimated, become accustomed to your profession in a small place, before you launch out in a city," his father had said, and the son had acquiesced. It was the natural wing-trying process before large flights were attempted, and the course commended itself to his reason. James, as well as his father, had good reasoning power. He whistled to himself as he walked along. He was very happy. He had a sensation as of one who has his goal in sight. He thought of his father, his mother, and his two younger sisters, but with no distress at absenting himself from them, although he lived in accord with his family. Twenty-five miles to his joyous youth seemed but as a step across the road. He had no sense of separation. "What is twenty-five miles?" he had said laughingly to his mother, when she had kissed him good-by. He had no conception of her state of mind with regard to the break in the home circle. He who was the breaker did not even see the break. Therefore he walked along, conscious of an immense joy in his own soul, and wholly unconscious of anything except joy in the souls of those whom he had left behind. It was a glorious morning, a white morning. The ground was covered with white frost, the trees, the house-roofs, the very air, were all white. In the west a transparent moon was slowly sinking; the east deepened with red and violet tints. Then came the sun, upheaving above the horizon like a ship of glory, and all the whiteness burned, and glowed, and radiated jewel-lights. James looked about with the delight of a discoverer. It might have been his first morning. He begun to meet men going to their work, swinging tin dinner-pails. Even these humble pails became glorified, they gave back the sunlight like burnished silver. He smelled the odors of breakfast upon the men's clothes. He held up his head high with a sort of good-humored arrogance as he passed. He would have fought to the death for any one of these men, but he knew himself, quite innocently, upon superior heights of education, and trained thought, and ambition. He met a man swinging a pail; he was coughing: a wretched, long rattle of a cough. James stopped him, opened his little medicine-case, and produced some pellets.

"Here, take one of these every hour until the cough is relieved, my friend," said he.

The man stared, swallowed a pellet, stared again, in an odd, suspicious, surly fashion, muttered something unintelligible and passed on.

There were three villages between Gresham and Alton: Red Hill, Stanbridge, and Westover. James stopped in Red Hill at a quick-lunch wagon, which was drawn up on the principal street under the lee of the town hall, went in, ordered and ate with relish some hot frankfurters, and drank some coffee. He had eaten a plentiful breakfast before starting, but the keen air had created his appetite anew. Beside him at the counter sat a young workingman, also eating frankfurters and drinking coffee. Now and then he gave a sidelong and supercilious glance at James's fine clothes. James caught one of the glances, and laughed good-naturedly.

"These quick-lunch wagons are a mighty good idea," said he.

The man grunted and took a swallow of coffee.

"Where do you work?" asked James.

"None of your damn business!" retorted the other man unexpectedly. "Where do you work yourself?"

James stared at him, then he burst into a roar. For a second the man's surly mouth did not budge, then the corners twitched a little.

"What in thunder are you mad about?" inquired James. "I am going to work for Doctor Gordon in Alton, and I don't care a damn where you work." James spoke with the most perfect good nature, still laughing.

Then the man's face relaxed into a broad grin. "Didn't know but you were puttin' on lugs," said he. "I am about tired of all those damned benefactors comin' along and arskin' of a man whot's none of their business, when a man knows all the time they don't care nothin' about it, and then makin' a man take somethin' he don't want, so as to get their names in the papers." The man sniffed a sniff of fury, then his handsome blue eyes smiled pleasantly, even with mischievous confidence into James's, and he swallowed more coffee.

"I am no benefactor, you can bet your life on that," said James. "I don't mean to give you anything you want or don't want."

"Didn't know but you was one of that kind," returned the man.

"Why?"

The man eyed James's clothes expressively.

"Oh, you mean my clothes," said James. "Well, this suit and overcoat are pretty fair, but if I were a benefactor I should be wearing seedy clothes, and have my wallet stuffed with bills for other folks."

"You bet you wouldn't," said the other man. "That ain't the way benefactors go to work. What be you goin' to do at Doc Gordon's?"

"Drive," replied James laconically.

"Guess you can't take care of hosses in no sech togs as them."

"I've got some others. I'm going to learn to doctor a little, too, if I can."

The man surveyed him, then he burst into a great laugh. "Well," said he, "when I git the measles I'll call you in."

"All right," said James, "I won't charge you a red cent. I'll doctor you and all your children and your wife for nothing."

"Guess you won't need to charge nothin' for the wife and kids, seein' as I ain't got none," said the man. "Ketch me saddled up with a woman an' kids, if I know what I'm about. Them's for the bene-factors. I live in a little shanty I rigged up myself out of two packin' boxes. I've got 'em on a man's medder here. He let me squat for nothin'. I git my meals here, an' I work on the railroad, an' I've got a soft snap, with nobody to butt in. Here, Mame, give us another cup of coffee. Mame's the girl I want, if I could hev one. Ain't you, Mame?"

The girl, who was a blonde, with an exaggerated pompadour fastened with aggressive celluloid pins, smiled pertly. "Reckon I h'ain't no more use for men than you hev for women," said she, as she poured the coffee. All that could be seen of her behind the counter was her head, and her waist clad in a red blouse, pinned so high to her skirt in the rear that it almost touched her shoulder blades. The blouse was finished at the neck with a nice little turn-over collar fastened with a brooch set with imitation diamonds and sapphires.

"Now, Mame, you know," said the man with assumed pathos, "that it is only because I'm a poor devil that I don't go kerflop the minute I set eyes on you. But you wouldn't like to live in boxes, would you? Would you now?"

"Not till my time comes, and not in boxes, then, less I'm in a railroad accident," replied the girl, with ghastly jocularity.

"She's got another feller, or *you* might git her if you've got a stiddy job," the man said, winking at James with familiarity.

"Just my luck," said James. He looked at the girl, and thought her pretty and pathetic, with a vulgar, almost tragic, prettiness and pathos. She was anaemic and painfully thin. Her blouse was puffed out over her flat chest. She looked worn out with the miserable little tediums of life, with constant stepping over ant-hills of stu-pidity and petty hopelessness. Her work was not, comparatively speaking, arduous, but the serving of hot coffee and frankfurters to workingmen was not progressive, and she looked as if her prin-cipal diet was the left-overs of the stock in trade. She seemed to exhale an odor of musty sandwiches and sausages and muddy coffee.

The man swallowed his second cup in fierce gulps. He glanced at his Ingersoll watch. "Gee whiz!" said he. "It's time I was off! Good-by, Mame."

The girl turned her head with a toss, and did not reply. "Good-by," James said.

The man grinned. "Good-by, Doc," he said. "I'll call you when I git the measles. You're a good feller. If you'd been a benefactor I'd run you out."

The man clattered down the steps of the gaudily painted little structure. The girl whom he had called Mame turned and looked at James with a sort of innocent boldness. "He's a queer feller," she observed.

"He seems to be."

"He is, you bet. Livin' in a house he's built out of boxes when he makes big money. He's on strike every little while. I wouldn't look at him. Don't know what he's drivin' at half the time. Reckon he's—" She touched her head significantly.

"Lots of folks are," said James affably.

"That's so." She stared reflectively at James. "I'm keepin' this quick lunch 'cause my father's sick," said she. "I see a lot of human nature in here."

"I suppose you do."

"You bet. Every kind gits in here first and last, tramps up to swells who think they're doin' somethin' awful funny to git frankfurters and coffee in here. They must be hard driv."

"I suppose they are sometimes."

Mame's eyes, surveying James, suddenly grew sharp. "You ain't one?" she asked accusingly.

"You bet not."

Mame's eyes grew soft. "I knew you were all right," said she. "Sometimes they say things to me that their fine lady friends would bounce 'em for, but I knew the minute I saw you that you wasn't that kind if you be dressed up like a gent. Reckon you've been makin' big money in your last place."

"Considerable," admitted James. He felt like a villain, but he had not the heart to accuse himself of being a gentleman before this pathetic girl.

Mame leaned suddenly over the counter, and her blonde crest

nearly touched his forehead. "Say," said she, in a whisper.

"What?" whispered James back.

"What he said ain't true. There ain't a mite of truth in it."

"What he said," repeated James vaguely.

Mame pouted. "How awful thick-headed you be," said she. "What he said about my havin' a feller." She blushed rosily, and her eyes fell.

James felt his own face suffused. He pulled out his pocket-book, and rose abruptly. "I'm sorry," he said with stupidity.

The rosy flush died away from the girl's face. "Nobody asked you to be sorry," said she. "I could have any one of a dozen I know if I jest held out my little finger."

"Of course, you could," James said. He felt apologetic, although he did not know exactly why. He fumbled over the change, and at last made it right with a quarter extra for the girl.

"It's a quarter too much," said she.

"Keep it, please."

She hesitated. She was frowning under her great blonde roll, her mouth looked hurt.

"What a fuss about a quarter," said James, with a laugh. "Keep it. That's a good girl."

Mame took a dingy handkerchief out of the bosom of her blouse, untied a corner, and James heard a jingle of coins meeting. Then she laughed. "You're an awful fraud," said she.

"Why?"

"You can't cheat me, if you did Bill Slattery."

"I think I don't know what you mean."

"You're a gent."

The girl's thin, coarse laughter rang out after James as he descended the steps of the quick-lunch wagon. She opened the door directly after he had closed it, and stood on the top step with the cold wind agitating her fair hair. "Say," she called after him.

James turned as he walked away. "What is it?"

"Nothin', only I was foolin' you, and so was Bill. I've got a feller, and Bill's him."

"I'll make you a present when you're married," James called back with a laugh.

"It's to come off next summer," cried the girl.

"I won't forget," answered James. He knew the girl lied; that she was not about to marry the workingman. He said to himself, as he strode on refreshed with his coarse fare, that girls were extraordinary: first they were bold to positive indecency, then modest to the borders of insanity.

James walked on. He reached Stanbridge about noon. Then he was hungry again. There was a good hotel there, and he made a substantial meal. He had a smoke and a rest of half an hour, then he resumed his walk. He soon passed the outskirts of Stanbridge, which was a small, old city, then he was in the country. The houses were sparsely set well back from the road. He met nobody, except an occasional countryman driving a wood-laden team. Presently the road lay between stately groves of oaks, although now and then they stood on one side only of the highway. Nearly all the oaks bore a shag of dried leaves about their trunks, like mossy beards of old men, only the shag was a bright russet instead of white. The ground under the oaks was like cloth-of-gold under the sun, the fallen leaves yet retained so much color. James heard a sharp croak, then a crow flew with wide flaps of dark wings across the road and perched on an oak bough. It cocked its head, and watched him wisely. James whistled at it, but it did not stir. It remained with its head cocked in that attitude of uncanny wisdom.

Suddenly James saw before him the figure of a girl, moving swiftly. She must have come out of the wood. She went as freely as a woodland thing, although she was conventionally dressed in a tailor suit of brown. Her hat, too, was brown, and a brown feather curled over the brim. She walked fast, with evidently as much enjoyment of the motion as James himself. They both walked like winged things.

Suddenly James had a queer experience. One sense became transposed into another, as one changes the key in music. He heard absolutely nothing, but it was as if he saw a noise. He saw a man standing on the right between him and the girl. The man had not made the slightest sound, he was sure. James had good ears, but sound and not sight was what betrayed him, or rather sound transposed into sight. He stood as motionless as a tree himself. James knew that he had been looking at the girl. Now she was looking at him. James felt a long shudder creep over him. He had never been afraid of anything except fear. Now he was afraid of fear, and there was something about the man which awakened this terror, yet it was inexplicable. He was a middle-aged man, and distinctly handsome. He was something above the medium height, and very well dressed. He wore a fur-lined coat which looked opulent. He had gray hair and a black mustache. There was nothing menacing in his face. He was, indeed, smiling a curious retrospective smile, as if at his own thoughts. Although his eyes regarded James attentively, this smiling mouth seemed entirely oblivious of him. The man gave an odd impression, as of two personalities: the one observant, with an animal-like observance for his own weal or woe, the other observant with intelligence. It was possibly this impression of a dual personality which gave James his quick sense of horror. He walked on, feeling his very muscles shrink. Just before James reached the man he emerged easily, with not the slightest appearance of stealth, from the wood, and walked on before him with a rapid, swinging stride. There were then three persons upon the road: the girl in brown, the strange man in the fur-lined coat, and James Elliot. James quickened his pace, but the other man kept ahead of him, and reached the girl. He stopped and James broke into a run. He saw the man place a hand upon the girl's shoulder, and make a motion as if to turn her face toward his. James came up with a shout, and the man disappeared abruptly, with a quick backward glance at James, into the wood.

The girl looked at James, and her little face under her brown plumed hat was very white. "Oh," she gasped, as if she had always known him, "I am so glad you are here! He frightened me terribly."

She tried to smile at James, although her poor little mouth was quivering. "Who was he?" she asked.

"I don't know."

A sudden suspicion flashed into her eyes. "He wasn't with you?"

"No. I saw him on the edge of the woods back there, and I didn't like his looks. When he started to follow you I hurried to catch up."

"Oh, thank you," said the girl fervently. "Do forgive me for asking if you were with him. I knew you were not the minute I saw you. I did not turn my face, although he tried to make me. I don't know why, but I do know he was something terrible and wicked." The girl said this last with a shudder. She caught hold of James's arm innocently, as a frightened child might have done. "You don't think he will come back?"

"No, and if he does I will take care of you."

"He may be—armed."

Suddenly the girl reeled. "Don't let me faint away. I won't faint away," she said in an angry voice. James saw that she was actually biting her lips to overcome the faintness.

"If you will sit down on that rock for a moment," said James, "I have something in my medicine-case which will revive you. I am a doctor."

"I shall faint away if I sit down and give up to it, if I swallow your whole case," said the girl weakly. "I know myself. Let me hold your arm and walk, and don't make me talk, then I can get over it." She was biting her lips almost to bleeding.

James walked on as he was bidden, with the slender little brown-clad figure clinging to him. He realized that he had fallen in with a girl who had a will which was possibly superior to anything in his medicine-case when it came to overcoming fright.

They walked on until they came in sight of a farm-house, when the girl spoke again, and James saw that the color was returning to her face. "I am all right now," said she, and withdrew her hand from his arm. She gave her head an angry, whimsical shake. "I am ashamed of myself," said she, "but I was horribly frightened, and sometimes I do faint. I can generally get the better of myself, but sometimes I can't. It always makes me so angry. I do hope you don't think I am such an awful coward, because I am not."

"I think most girls whom I have known would have made much more fuss than you did," said James. "You never screamed."

"I never did scream in my life," said the girl. "I don't think I could. I don't know how. I think if I did scream, I should certainly faint."

James stopped and opened his medicine-case. "I think you had better take just a swallow of brandy," said he.

The girl thrust back the bottle which he offered her with high disdain. "Brandy," said she, "just because I have been frightened a little! I should be ashamed of myself if I did such a thing. I am ashamed now for almost fainting away, but I should never forgive myself if I took brandy because of it. If I haven't nerve enough to keep straight without brandy, I should be a pretty poor specimen of a girl." She looked at him indignantly, and James saw what he had not seen before (he had been so engrossed with the strangeness of the situation), that she was a beautiful girl with a singular type of beauty. She was very small, but she gave the impression of intense springiness and wiriness. Although she was thin, no one could have called her delicate. She looked as much alive as a flame, with nerves on the surface from head to heel. Her eyes were blue, not large, but full of light, her hair, which tossed around her face in a soft fluff, was ash-blonde. Brown was the last color, theoretically, which she should have worn, but it suited her. The ash and brown, the two neutral tints, served to bring out the blue fire of her eyes and the intense red of her lips. However, her beauty lay not so much in her regular features as in the wonderful flame-like quality which animated them, and which they assumed when she spoke or listened. In repose, her face was as neutral as a rock or dead leaf. It was neither beautiful nor otherwise. When it was animated, it was as if the rock gave out silver lights of mica and rosy crystal under strong light, and as if the dead leaf leapt into flame. James thought her much prettier than any of his sisters or their friends, but he was led quite unknowingly into this opinion, because of his own position as her protector. That made him realize his own male gorgeousness and strength, and he really saw the girl with such complacency instead of himself.

They walked along, and all at once he stopped short. Something occurred to him, which, strange to say, had not occurred before. He was not in the least cowardly. He was brave almost to foolhardiness. All at once it occurred to him that he ought to follow the man.

"Good Lord!" said he and stopped.

"What is the matter?" asked the girl.

"Why, I must follow that man. He is a suspicious character. He ought not to be left at large."

"I suppose you don't care if you leave me alone," said the girl accusingly.

James stared at her doubtfully. There was that view of the situation.

"I am going to see my friend Annie Lipton, who lives in Westover. There is half a mile of lonely road before I get there. That man, for all I know, may be keeping sight of us in the woods over there. While you are going back to chase him, he may come up with me. Well, run along if you want to. I am not afraid." But the girl's lips quivered, and she paled again.

James glanced at the stretch of road ahead. There was not a house in sight. Woods were on one side, on the other was a rolling expanse of meadowland covered with dried last year's grass, like coarse oakum-colored hair.

"I think I had better keep on with you," James said.

"You can do exactly as you choose," the girl replied defiantly, but tremulously. "I am not in the least dependent upon men to escort me. I wander miles around by myself. This is the first time I have seemed to be in the slightest danger. I dare say there was no danger this time, only he came up behind like a cat, and—"

"He didn't say anything?"

"No, he didn't speak. He only tried to make me turn my head, so he could see my face, and directly it seemed to me that I must die rather than let him. He was trying to make me turn my head. I think maybe he was an insane man."

"I will go on with you," said James.

They walked on for the half mile of which the girl had spoken. A sudden shyness seemed to have come over both of them. Then they began to come in sight of houses. "I am not afraid now," said the girl, "but I do think you are very foolish if you go back alone and try to hunt that man. Ten chances to one he is armed, and you haven't a thing to defend yourself with, except that medicine-case."

"I have my fists," replied James indignantly.

"Fists don't count much against a revolver."

"Well, I am going to try," said James with emphasis.

"Good-by, then. You are treating me shamefully, though."

James stared at her in amazement. She was actually weeping, tears were rolling over her cheeks.

"What do you mean?" said he. "Don't feel so badly."

"You can't be very quick-witted not to see. If you should meet that man, and get killed, I should really be the one who killed you and not the man."

"Why, no, you would not."

The girl stamped her foot. "Yes, I should, too," said she, half-sobbing. "You would not have been killed except for me. You know you would not."

She spoke as if she actually saw the young man dead before her, and was indignant because of it, and he burst into a peal of laughter.

"Laugh if you want to," said she. "It does not seem to me any laughing matter to go and get yourself killed by me, and my having that on my mind my whole life. I think I should go mad." Her voice shook, an expression of horror came into her blue eyes.

James laughed again. "Very well, then," he said, "to oblige you I won't get killed."

He, in fact, began to consider that the day was waning, and what a wild-goose chase it would probably be for him to attempt to follow the man. So again they walked on until they reached the main street of Westover.

Westover was a small village, rather smaller than Gresham. They passed three gin-mills, a church, and a grocery store. Then the girl stopped at the corner of a side street. "My friend lives on this street," said she. "Thank you very much. I don't know what I should have done if you had not come. Good-by!" She went so quickly that James was not at all sure that she heard his answering good-by. He thought again how very handsome she was. Then he began to wonder where she lived, and how she would get home from her friend's house, if the friend had a brother who would escort her. He wondered who her friends were to let a girl like that wander around alone in a State which had not the best reputation for safety. He entertained the idea of waiting about until she left her friend's house, then he considered the possible brother, and that the girl herself might resent it, and he kept on. The western sky was putting on wonderful tints of cowslip and rose deepening into violet. He began considering his own future again, relegating the girl to the background. He must be nearing Alton, he thought. After a three-mile stretch of farming country, he saw houses again. Lights were gleaming out in the windows. He heard wheels, and the regular trot of a horse behind him, then a mud-bespattered buggy passed him, a shabby buggy, but a strongly built one. The team of horses was going at a good clip. James stood on one side, but the team and buggy had no sooner passed than he heard a whoa! and a man's face peered around the buggy wing, not at James, but at his medicine-case. James could just discern the face, bearded and shadowy in the gathering gloom. Then a voice came. It shouted, one word, the expressive patois of the countryside, that word which may be at once a question and a salute, may express almost any emotion. "Halloo!" said the voice.

This halloo involved a question, or so James understood it. He quickened his pace, and came alongside the buggy. The face, more distinct now, surveyed him, its owner leaning out over the side of the buggy. "Who are you? Where are you bound?"

James answered the latter question. "I am going to Alton."

"To Doctor Gordon's?"

"Yes."

"Then you are Doctor Elliot?"

"Yes."

"Get in."

James climbed into the buggy. The other man took up the reins, and the horse resumed his quick trot.

"You didn't come by train?" remarked the man.

"No. You are Doctor Gordon, I suppose?"

"Yes, I am. Why the devil did you walk?"

"To save my money," replied James, laughing. He realized nothing to be ashamed of in his reply.

"But I thought your father was well-to-do."

"Yes, he is, but we don't ride when it costs money and we can walk. I knew if I got to Alton by night, it would be soon enough. I like to walk." James said that last rather defiantly. He began to realize a certain amazement on the other man's part which might amount to an imputation upon his father. "I have plenty of money in my pocket," he added, "but I wanted the walk."

Doctor Gordon laughed. "Oh, well, a walk of twenty-five miles is nothing to a young fellow like you, of course," he said. "I can understand that you may like to stretch your legs. But you'll have to drive if you are ever going to get anywhere when you begin practice with me."

"I suppose you have calls for miles around?"

"Rather." Doctor Gordon sighed. "It's a dog's life. I suppose you haven't got that through your head yet?"

"I think it is a glorious profession," returned James, with his haughty young enthusiasm.

"I wasn't talking about the profession," said the doctor; "I was talking of the man who has to grind his way through it. It's a dog's life. Neither your body nor your soul are your own. Oh, well, maybe you'll like it."

"You seem to," remarked James rather pugnaciously.

"I? What can I do, young man, but stick to it whether I like it or not? What would they do? Yes, I suppose I am fool enough to like a dog's life, or rather to be unwilling to leave it. No money could induce me anyhow. I suppose you know there is not much money in it?"

James said that he had not supposed a fortune was to be made in a country practice.

"The last bill any of them will pay is the doctor's," said Doctor Gordon. Then he added with a laugh, "especially when the doctor is myself. They have to pay a specialist from New York, but I wait until they are underground, and the relatives, I find, stick faster to the monetary remains than the bark to a tree. If I hadn't a little private fortune, and my—sister a little of her own, I expect we should starve."

James noticed with a little surprise the doctor's hesitation before he spoke of his sister. It seemed then that he was not married. Somehow, James had thought of him as married as a matter of course.

Doctor Gordon hastened to explain, as if divining the other's attitude. "I dare say you don't know anything about my family relations," said he. "My widowed sister, Mrs. Ewing, keeps house for me. I live with her and her daughter. I think you will like them both, and I think they will like you, though I'll be hanged if I have grasped anything of you so far but your medicine-case and your voice. Your voice is all right. You give yourself away by it, and I always like that."

James straightened himself a little. There was something bantering in the other's tone. It made him feel young, and he resented being made to feel young. He himself at that time felt older than he ever would feel again. He realized that he was not being properly estimated. "If," said he, with some heat, "a patient can make out anything by my voice as to what I think, I miss my guess."

"I dare say not," said Doctor Gordon, and his own voice was as if he put the matter aside.

He spoke to the horse, whose trot quickened, and they went on in silence.

At last James began to feel rather ashamed of himself. He unstiffened. "I had quite an exciting and curious experience after I left Stanbridge," said he.

"Did you?" said the other in an absent voice.

James went on to relate the matter in detail. His companion turned an intent face upon him as he proceeded. "How far back was it?" he asked, and his tone was noticeably agitated.

"Just after I left the last house in Stanbridge. We went on together to Westover. She mentioned something about going to see a friend there. I think Lipton was the name, and she left me suddenly."

"What was the girl like?"

"Small and slight, and very pretty."

"Dressed in brown?"

"Yes."

"How did the man look?" Doctor Gordon's voice fairly alarmed the young man.

"I hardly can say. I saw him distinctly, but only for a second. The impression he gave me was of a middle-aged man, although he looked young."

"Good-looking?"

"My God, no!" said James, as the man's face seemed to loom up before him again. "He looked like the devil."

"A man may look like the devil, and yet be distinctly handsome."

"Well, I suppose he was; but give me the homeliest face on earth rather than a face like that man's, if I must needs have anything to do with him." The young fellow's voice broke. He was very young. He caught the other man by his rough coat sleeve. "See here, Doctor Gordon," said he, "my profession is to save life. That is the main end of it but, but—I don't honestly know what I should think right, if I were asked to save *that* man's life."

"Was he well dressed?"

"More than well dressed, richly, a fur-lined coat—"

"Tall?"

"Yes, above the medium, but he stooped a little, like a cat, sort of stretched to the ground like an animal, when he hurried along after the girl in front of me."

Doctor Gordon struck the horse with his whip, and he broke into a gallop. "We are almost home," said he. "I shall have to leave you with slight ceremony. I have to go out again immediately."

Doctor Gordon had hardly finished speaking before they drew up in front of a white house on the left of the road. "Get out," he said peremptorily to James. The front door opened, and a parallelogram of lighted interior became visible. In this expanse of light stood a tall woman's figure. "Clara, this is the new doctor," called out Doctor Gordon. "Take him in and take care of him."

"Have you got to go away again?" said the woman's voice. It was sweet and rich, but had a curious sad quality in it.

"Yes, I must. I shall not be gone long. Don't wait supper."

"Aren't you going to change the horse?"

"Can't stop. Go right in, Elliot. Clara, look after him."

James Elliot found himself in the house, confronting the most beautiful woman he had ever seen, as the rapid trot of the doctor's horse receded in vistas of sound.

James almost gasped. He had never seen such a woman. He had seen pretty girls. Now he suddenly realized that a girl was not a woman, and no more to be compared with her than an uncut gem with one whose facets take the utmost light.

The boy stood staring at this wonderful woman. She extended her hand to him, but he did not see it. She said some gracious words of greeting to him, but he did not hear them. She might have been the Venus de Milo for all he heard or realized of sentient life in her. He was rapt in contemplation of herself, so rapt that he was oblivious of her. She smiled. She was accustomed to having men, especially very young men, take such an attitude on first seeing her. She did not wait any longer, but herself took the young man's hand, and drew him gently into the room, and spoke so insistently that she compelled him to leave her and attend. "I suppose you are Doctor Gordon's assistant?" she said.

James relapsed into the tricks of his childhood. "Yes, ma'am," he replied. Then he blushed furiously, but the woman seemed to notice neither the provincial term nor his confusion. He found himself somehow, he did not know how, divested of his overcoat, and the vision had disappeared, having left some words about dinner ringing in his ears, and he was sitting before a hearth-fire in a large leather easy-chair. Then he looked about the room in much the same dazed fashion in which he had contemplated the woman. He had never seen a room like it. He was used to conventionality, albeit richness, and a degree even of luxury. Here were absolute unconventionality, richness, and luxury of a kind utterly strange to him. The room was very large and long, extending nearly the whole length of the house. There were many windows with Eastern rugs instead of curtains. There were Eastern things hung on the walls which gave out dull gleams of gold and silver and topaz and turquoise. There were a great many books on low shelves. There were bronzes, jars, and squat idols. There were a few pieces of Chinese ivory work. There were many skins of lions, bears, and tigers on the floor, besides a great Persian rug which gleamed like a blurred jewel. Besides the firelight there was only one great bronze lamp to illuminate the room. This lamp had a red shade, which cast a soft, fiery glow over everything. There were not many pictures. The rich Eastern stuffs, and even a skin or two of tawny hue, covered most of the wall-spaces above the book-cases, giving backgrounds of color to bronzes and ivory carvings, but there was one picture at the farther end of the room which attracted James's notice. All that he could distinguish from where he sat was a splash of splendid red.

He gazed, and his curiosity grew. Finally he rose, traversed the room, and came close to the picture. It was a portrait of the woman who had met him at the door. The red was the red of a splendid robe of velvet. The portrait was evidently the work of no mean artist. The texture of the velvet was something wonderful, so were the flesh tones; but James missed something in the face. The portrait had been painted, he knew instinctively, before some great change had come into the woman's heart, which had given her another aspect of beauty.

James turned away. Then he noticed something else which seemed rather odd about the room. All the windows were furnished with heavy wooden shutters, and, early as it was, hardly dark, all were closed, and fastened securely. James somehow got an impression of secrecy, that it was considered necessary that no glimpse of the interior should be obtained from without after the lamp was lit. They sat often carelessly at his own home of an evening with the shades up, and all the interior of the room plainly visible from the road. An utter lack of secrecy was in James's own character. He scowled a little, as he returned to his seat by the fire. He was too confused to think clearly, but he was conscious of a certain homesickness for the wonted things of his life, when the door opened and the woman reëntered.

James rose, and she spoke in her sweet voice. It was rather lower pitched than the voices of most women, and had a resonant quality. "Your room is quite ready, Doctor Elliot," said she. "Your trunk is there. If you would like to go there before dinner, I will pilot you. We have but one maid, and she is preparing the dinner, which will be ready as soon as you are. I hope Doctor Gordon and Clemency will have returned by that time, too."

By Clemency James understood that she meant her daughter, of whom Doctor Gordon had spoken. He wondered at the unusual name, as he followed his hostess. His room was on the same floor as the living-room. She threw open a door at the other side of the hall, and James saw an exceedingly comfortable apartment with a hearth-fire, with book-shelves, and a couch-bed covered with a rug, and a desk. "I thought you would prefer this room," said the woman. "There are others on the second floor, but this has the advantage of your being able to use it as a sitting-room, and you may like to have your friends, whom I trust you will find in Alton, come in from time to time. You will please make yourself quite at home."

James had not yet fairly comprehended the beauty of the woman. He was still too dazzled. Had he gone away at that time, he could not for the life of him have described her, but he did glance, as a woman might have done, at her gown. It was of a soft heavy red silk, trimmed with lace, and was cut out in a small square at the throat. This glimpse of firm white throat made James wonder as to evening costume for himself. At home he never dreamed of such a thing, but here it might be different. His hostess divined his thoughts. She smiled at him as if he were a child. "No," said she, "you do not need to dress for dinner. Doctor Gordon never does when we are by ourselves."

Then she went away, closing the door softly after her.

James noticed that over the windows of this room were only ordinary shades, and curtains of some soft red stuff. There were no shutters. He looked about him. He was charmed with his room, and it did away to a great extent with his feeling of homesickness. It was not unlike what his room at college had been. It was more like all rooms. He had no feeling of the secrecy which the great living-room gave him, and which irritated him. He brushed his clothes and his hair, and washed his hands and face. While he was doing so he heard wheels and a horse's fast trot. He guessed immediately that the doctor had returned. He therefore, as soon as he had completed the slight changes in his toilet, started to return to the living-room. Crossing the hall he met Doctor Gordon, who seized him by the shoulder, and whispered in his ear, "Not a word before Mrs. Ewing about what happened this afternoon."

James nodded. "More mystery," thought he with asperity.

"You have not spoken of it to her already, I hope," said Doctor Gordon with quick anxiety.

"No, I have not. I have scarcely seen her."

"Well, not a word, I beg of you. She is very nervous."

The doctor had been removing his overcoat and hat. When he had hung them on some stag's horn in the hall, he went with James into the living-room.

There, beside the fire, sat the girl in brown whom James had met that afternoon on the road.

CHAPTER II

She looked up when he entered, and there was in her young girl face the very slightest shade of recognition. She could not help it, for Clemency was candor itself. Then she bowed very formally, and shook hands sedately when Doctor Gordon introduced James as Doctor Elliot, his new assistant, and carried off her part very well. James was not so successful. He colored and was somewhat confused, but nobody appeared to notice it. Clemency went on relating how glad she was that Uncle Tom met her as she was coming home from Annie Lipton's. "I am never afraid," said she, and her little face betrayed the lie, "but I was tired, and besides I was beginning to be cold, for I went out without my fur."

"You should not have gone without it. It grows so cold when the sun goes down," said Mrs. Ewing. Then a chime of Japanese bells was heard which announced dinner.

"Doctor Elliot will be glad of dinner," said Doctor Gordon. "He has walked all the way from Gresham."

Clemency looked at him with approval, and tried to look as if she had never seen him walking in her life. "That is a good walk," said she. "Twenty-five miles it must be. If more men walked instead of working poor horses all the time, it would be better for them."

"That is a hint for your Uncle Tom," said Gordon laughingly.

"I never hint," said Clemency. "It is just a plain statement. Men are walking animals. They could travel as well as horses in the course of time if they only put their minds to it."

"Well, your old uncle's bones must be saved, even at the expense of the horse's," said Doctor Gordon.

"Bones are improved by use," said Clemency severely, as she took her seat at the dinner-table. They all laughed. The girl herself relaxed her pretty face with a whimsical smile. It was quite evident that Clemency was the spoiled and petted darling of the house, and that she traded innocently upon the fact. The young doctor, although his first impression of the elder woman was still upon him, yet realized the charm of the young girl. The older woman was, as it were, crowned with an aureole of perfection, but the young girl was crowned with possibilities which dazzled with mystery. She looked prettier, now that her outer garments were removed, and her thick crown of ash-blonde hair was revealed. The lamp lit her eyes into bluer flame. She was a darling of a young girl, and more a darling because she had the sweetest confidence in everybody thinking her one.

However, James Elliot, sitting in the well-appointed dining-room, which was more like a city house than a little New Jersey dwelling, did not for a second retreat from his first impression of Mrs. Ewing. Behind the coffee-urn sat the woman with whom he had not fallen in love, that was too poor a term to use. He had become a worshipper. He felt himself, body and soul, prostrate before the Divinity of Womanhood itself. He realized the grandeur of the abstract in the individual. What was any spoiled, sweet young girl to that? And Mrs. Ewing was, in truth, a wonderful creature. She was a large woman with a great quantity of blue-black hair, which had the ripples one sees in antique statues. Her eyes, black at first glance, were in reality dark blue. Her face gave one a never-ending surprise. James had not known that a woman could be so beautiful. Vague comparisons with the Greek Helen, or Cleopatra, came into his head. Now and then he stole a glance at her. He dared not often. She did not talk much, but he was rather pleased with that fact, although her voice was so sweet and gracious. Speech in a creature like that was not an essential. It might even be an excrescence upon a perfection. It did not occur to the dazed mind of her worshipper that Mrs. Ewing might have very simple and ordinary reasons for not talking—that she might be tired or ill, or preoccupied. But after a number of those stolen glances, James discovered with a great pang, as if one should see for the first time that the arms of the Venus were really gone, when his fancy had supplied them, that the woman did not look well. In spite of her beauty, there was ill-health evident in her face. James was a mere tyro in his profession as yet, but certain infallible signs were there which he could not mistake. They were the signs of suffering, possibly of very great suffering. She ate very little, James noticed, although she made a pretense of eating as much as any one. James saw that Doctor Gordon also noticed it. When the maid was taking away Mrs. Ewing's plate, he spoke with a gruffness which astonished the young man. "For Heaven's sake, why don't you eat your dinner, Clara?" said he. "Emma, replace Mrs. Ewing's plate. Now, Clara, eat your dinner." To James's utter astonishment, Mrs. Ewing obeyed like a child. She ate every morsel, although she could not restrain her expression of loathing. When the salad and dessert were brought on she ate them also.

Doctor Gordon watched her with what seemed, to the young man, positive brutality. His mouth under his heavy beard quivered perceptibly whenever he looked at his sister eating, his forehead became corrugated, and his deep-set eyes sparkled. James was heartily glad when dinner was over, and, at Doctor Gordon's request, he followed him into his office.

Doctor Gordon's office was a small room at the back of the house. It had an outer door communicating with a path which led to the stable. Two sides of the room were lined with medical books, and two with bottles containing diverse colored mixtures. A hanging lamp was over the center of a long table in the middle of the room. Around it dangled prisms, which cast rainbow colors over everything. The first thing which struck one on entering the room was the extraordinary color scheme: the dull gleams of the books, the medicine bottles which had lights like jewels, and over all the flickers of prismatic hues. The long table was covered with corks, empty bottles, books, a medicine-case, and newspapers, besides a mighty inkstand and writing materials. There were also a box of cigars, a great leather tobacco pouch, and, interspersed among all, a multitude of pipes. The doctor drew a chair beside this chaotic table lit with rainbow lights, and invited James to sit down. "Sit down a moment," he said. "Will you have a pipe or a cigar?"

"Cigar, please," replied James. The doctor pushed the box toward him. James realized immediately a ten-cent cigar at the least when he began to smoke. Doctor Gordon filled a pipe mechanically. His face still wore the gloomy, almost fierce, expression which it had assumed at table. He was a handsome man in a rough, sketchy fashion. His face was blurred with a gray grizzle of beard. He wore his hair rather long, and he had a fashion of running his fingers through it, which made it look like a thick brush. He dressed rather carelessly, still like a gentleman. His clothes were slouchy, and needed brushing, but his linen was immaculate.

Doctor Gordon smoked in silence, which his young assistant was too shy to break. The elder man finished his pipe, then he rose with an impatient gesture and shook himself like a great shaggy dog. "Come, young man," said he, "we don't want to spend the evening like this. Get your hat and coat."

James obeyed, and the two men left the office by the outer door which opened on the stable. As they came around by the front of the house Clemency stood in the doorway.

"Are you going out, you and Doctor Elliot, Uncle Tom?" she called.

"Yes, dear; why?"

"Patients?"

"No; we are going down to Georgie K.'s. Tell your mother to go to bed at once."

When the two men were out in the street, walking briskly in the keen frosty air, James ventured a question. "Mrs. Ewing is not well, is she?" he said. He fairly started at the way in which his question was received. Doctor Gordon turned upon him even fiercely.

"She is perfectly well, perfectly well," he replied.

"She does not look—" began James.

"When you are as old as I am you can venture to diagnose on a woman's looks," said Gordon. "Clara is perfectly well."

James said no more. They walked on in silence under a pale sky. Above a low mountain range on their right was a faint light which indicated the coming of the moon. The ground was frozen in hard ridges. James walked behind the doctor on the narrow blue stone walk which served as sidewalk.

"This town has made no provision whatever for courting couples," said Doctor Gordon suddenly, and to James's astonishment his whole manner and voice had changed. It was far from gloomy. It was jocular even.

James laughed. "Yes, it would be difficult for two to walk arm in arm, however loving," he returned.

"Just so," said the doctor, "and the funny part of it is that this narrow sidewalk was intentional."

"Not for such a purpose?"

"Exactly so. It was given to the town by a rich spinster who died about twenty years ago. It was given in her will on condition that it should not be more than two feet wide."

"For that reason?"

"Just that reason. She had been jilted in her youth, and her heart had been wrung by the sight of her rival passing her very window where she sat watching for her lover, arm in arm with him. It was in summer, and the dirt sidewalk was dry. She made up her mind, then and there, that that sort of thing should be prevented."

They had just reached a handsome old house standing close to the narrow sidewalk. In fact, its windows opened directly upon it.

"This is the house," the doctor said in corroboration. James laughed, but he wondered within himself if he were being told fish tales. Doctor Gordon made him feel so very young that he resented it. He resented it the more when he realized the new glow of adoration in his heart for that older woman whom they had left behind. He began wondering about her: how much older she was. He said to himself that he did not care if she were old enough to be his mother, his grandmother even, there was no one in the whole world like her.

Then they came to the hotel, the Evarts House. It was rather pretentious, well built, with great columns in front supporting double verandas. It was also well lighted. It was evidently far above the usual order of a road house. Doctor Gordon entered, with James at his heels. They went into the great low room at the right of the door, which was the bar-room. Behind the bar stood an enormous man, yellow haired and yellow bearded, dispensing drinks. The whole low interior was dim with tobacco smoke, and scented with various liquors and spices. There was on one side a great fireplace, in which stood earthen pitchers, in which cider was being mulled with red-hot pokers, eager vinous faces watching. Nobody was intoxicated, but there was a general hum of hilarity and gusto of life about the place, an animal enjoyment of good cheer and jollity. It was in truth not respectable to get entirely drunk in Alton. It was genteel to become "set up," exhilarated, but the real gutter form of inebriety was frowned upon to a much greater extent than in many places where there was less license.

"Hullo!" sang out Doctor Gordon as he entered. Immediately a grin of comradeship overspread the pink face of the yellow-haired giant behind the bar. "Hullo!" he responded. "Just step into the other room, and I'll be there right away."

James followed Doctor Gordon into what was evidently the state parlor of the hotel. There was haircloth furniture, and a mahogany table, with various stains of conviviality upon its polished surface. There was a fire on the hearth, and on the mantel stood some gilded vases and a glass case of wax-flowers, also a stuffed canary under a glass shade, pathetic on his little twig. Doctor Gordon pointed to the flowers and the canary. "Poor old man lost his wife, when he had been married two years," he said. "She and the baby both died. That was before I came here. Damned if I wouldn't have pulled them through. That was her bird, and she made those fool flowers, poor little thing. I suppose if the hotel were to take fire Georgie K. would go for them before all the cash in the till."

"He hasn't married again?"

"Married again! It's my belief he'd shoot the man that mentioned it."

Then Georgie K. entered, his rosy face distended with a smile of the most intense hospitality, and before Doctor Gordon had a chance to introduce James, he said, "What'll you take, gentlemen?"

"This is my new assistant, from Gresham, Doctor Elliot," said Gordon. Georgie K. made a bow, and scraped his foot at the same time with a curiously boyish gesture. "What'll you take?" he asked again. That was evidently his formula of hospitality, which must never be delayed.

"Apple-jack," responded Doctor Gordon promptly. "You had better take apple-jack too, young man. Georgie K. has gin that beats the record, and peach brandy, but when it comes to his apple-jack—it's worth the whole State of New Jersey."

"All right," answered James.

Soon he found himself seated at the stained old mahogany table with the two men, and between two glasses, a bottle, and a pitcher of hot water. Doctor Gordon dealt a pack of dirty cards while the hotel keeper poured the apple-jack. James could not help staring at the elder doctor with more and more amazement. He seemed to assimilate perfectly with his surroundings. The tormented expression had gone from his face. He was simply convivial, and of the same sort as Georgie K. He no longer looked even a gentleman. He had become of the soil, the New Jersey soil. As they drank and played, he told stories, and roared with laughter at them. The stories also belonged to the soil, they were folk lore, wild, coarse, but full of humanity. Although Doctor Gordon drank freely of the rich mellow liquor, it did not apparently affect him. His cheeks above his gray furze of beard became slightly flushed, that was all.

James drank rather sparingly. The stuff seemed to him rather fiery, and he remembered the goddess in the doctor's house. He could imagine her look of high disdain at him should he return under the influence of liquor. Besides, he did not particularly care for the apple-jack.

It was midnight before they left. Georgie K. went to the door with them, and he and the doctor shook hands heartily. "Come again," said Georgie K., "and the sooner the better, and bring the young Doc. We'll make him have a good time."

Until they were near home, Doctor Gordon continued his strangely incongruous conversation, telling story after story, and shouting with laughter. When they came in sight of the house Gordon stopped suddenly and leaned against a great maple beside the road. He stared at the house, two of the upper windows of which were lighted, and gave a great sigh, almost a groan. James stopped also and stared at him. He wondered if the apple-jack had gone to the doctor's head after all. "What is the matter?" he ventured.

"Nothing, except the race is at a finish, and I am caught as I always am," replied Doctor Gordon.

"The race—" repeated James vaguely.

"Yes, the race with myself. Myself has caught up with me, God help me, and I am in its clutches. The time may come when you will try to race with self, my boy. Let me tell you, you will never win. You will tire yourself out, and make a damned idiot of yourself for nothing. I shall race again tomorrow. I never learn the lesson, but perhaps you can, you are young. Well, come along. Please be as quiet as you can when you go into the house. My sister may be asleep. She is perfectly well, but she is a little nervous. I need not repeat my request that you do not mention your adventure with Clemency this afternoon to her."

"Certainly not," said James. He walked on beside the doctor, and entered the house, more and more mystified. James was not sure, but he thought he heard the faintest little moan from upstairs. He glanced at Doctor Gordon's face, and it was again the face of the man whom he had seen before going to Georgie K.'s.

CHAPTER III

The next morning after breakfast, at which Mrs. Ewing did not appear, Doctor Gordon observed that she always took her rolls and coffee in bed. James followed Doctor Gordon into his office. Clemency, who had presided at the coffee urn, had done so silently, and looked, so James thought, rather sulky, as if something had gone wrong. Directly James was in the office, the doctor's man, Aaron, appeared. He was a tall, lank Jerseyman, incessantly chewing. His lean, yellow jaws appeared to have acquired a permanent rotary motion, but he had keen eyes of intelligence upon the doctor as he gave his orders.

"Put in the team," said Gordon. "We are going to Haver's Corner. Old Sam Edwards is pretty low, and I ought to have gone there yesterday, but I didn't know whether that child with diphtheria at Tucker's Mill would live the day out. Now he has seen the worst of it, thank the Lord! But today I must go to Haver's. I want to make good time, for there's something going on this afternoon, and I want an hour off if I can get it." Again the expression of simple jocularity was over the man's face, and James remembered what he had said the night before about again running a race with himself the next day.

After Aaron had gone out Gordon turned to James. He pointed to his great medicine-case on the table. "You might see to it that the bottles are all filled," he said. "You will find the medicines yonder." He pointed to the shelf. "I have to speak to Clemency before I go."

James obeyed. As he worked filling the bottles he heard dimly Gordon's voice talking to Clemency on the other side of the wall. The girl seemed to be expostulating.

When Doctor Gordon returned Aaron was at his heels with an immense bottle containing a small quantity of red fluid. "S'pose you'll want this filled?" he said to Gordon with a grin which only disturbed for a second his rotary jaws.

"Oh, yes, of course," replied Gordon, "we want the aqua."

James stared at him as he poured a little red-colored liquid from one of the bottles on the shelves into the big one. "Now fill it up from the pump, and put it in the buggy; be sure the cork is in tight," he said to Aaron.

Gordon looked laughingly at James when the man had gone. "I infer that you are wondering what 'aqua' may be," he said.

"I was brought up to think it was water," said James.

"So it is, water pure and simple, with a little coloring matter thrown in. Bless you, boy, the people around here want their medicines by the quart, and if they had them by the quart, good-by to the doctor's job, and ho for the undertaker! So the doctor is obliged to impose upon the credulity of the avariciously innocent, and dilute the medicine. Bless you, I have patients who would accuse me of cheating if I prescribed less than a cupful of medicine at a time. They have to be humored. After all, they are a harmless, good lot, but stiffened with hereditary ideas, worse than by rheumatism. If I should give a few drops in half a glass of water, and order a teaspoonful at a time, I should fly in the face of something which no mortal man can conquer, sheer heredity. The grandfathers and great-grandfathers of these people took their physic on draft, the children must do likewise. Sometimes I even think the medicine would lose its effect if taken in any other way. Nobody can estimate the power of a fixed idea upon the body. All the same, it is a confounded nuisance carrying around the aqua. I will confess, although I see the necessity of yielding, that I have less patience with men's stiff-necked stupidity than I have with their sins."

James drove all the morning with Doctor Gordon about the New Jersey country. It was a moist, damp day, such as sometimes comes even in winter. It was a dog day with an atmosphere slightly cooler than that of midsummer. Overcoats were oppressive, the horses steamed. The roads were deep with red mud, which clogged the wheels and made the hoofs of the horses heavy. "It's a damned soil," said Doctor Gordon. This morning after appearing somewhat saturnine at breakfast, he was again in his unnatural, rollicking mood. He hailed everybody whom he met. He joked with the patients and their relatives in the farmhouses, approached through cart-tracks of mire, and fluttered about by chickens, quacking geese, and dead leaves. Now and then, stately ranks of turkeys charged in line of battle upon the muddy buggy, and the team, being used to it, stood their ground, and snorted contemptuously. The country people were either saturnine with an odd shyness, which had something almost hostile in it, or they were effusively hospitable, forcing apple-jack upon the two doctors. James was much struck by the curious unconcern shown by the relatives of the patients, and even by the patients themselves. In only one case, and that of a child suffering from a bad case of measles, was much interest evinced. The majority of the patients were the very old and middle-aged, and they discussed, and heard discussed, their symptoms with much the same attitude as they might have discussed the mechanism of a wooden doll. If any emotion was shown it was that of a singular inverted pride. "I had a terrible night, doctor," said one old woman, and a smirk of self-conceit was over her ancient face. "Yes, mother *did* have an awful night," said her married daughter with a triumphant expression. Even the children clustering about the doctor looked unconsciously proud because their old grandmother had had an awful night. The call of the two doctors at the house was positively hilarious. Quantities of old apple-jack were forced upon them. The old woman in the adjoining bedroom, although she was evidently suffering, kept calling out a feeble joke in her cackling old voice.

"Those people seem positively elated because that old soul is sick," said James when he and the doctor were again in the buggy.

"They are," said Doctor Gordon, "even the old woman herself, who knows well enough that she has not long to live. Did you ever think that the desire of distinction was one of the most, perhaps the most, intense purely spiritual emotion of the human soul? Look at the way these people live here, grubbing away at the soil like ants. The most of them have in their lives just three ways of attracting notice, the momentary consideration of their kind: birth, marriage, sickness and death. With the first they are hardly actively concerned, even with the second many have nothing to do. There are more women than men as usual, and although the women want to marry, all the men do not. There remains only sickness and death for a stand-by, so to speak. If one of them is really sick and dies, the people are aroused to take notice. The sick person and the corpse have a certain state and dignity which they have never attained before. Why, bless you, man, I have one patient, a middle-aged woman, who has been laid up for years with rheumatism, and she is fairly vainglorious, and so is her mother. She brags of her invalid daughter. If she had been merely an old maid on her hands, she would have been ashamed of her, and the woman herself would have been sour and discontented. But she has fairly married rheumatism. It has been to her as a husband and children. I tell you, young man, one has to have his little footstool of elevation among his fellows, even if it is a mighty queer one, or he loses his self-respect, and self-respect is the best jewel we have."

They were now out in the road again, the team plodding heavily through the red shale. "It's a damned soil," said the doctor for the second time. He looked down at the young man beside him, and James again felt that resentful sense of youth and inexperience. "I don't know how you've been brought up," said the elder man. "I don't want to infuse heretic notions into your innocent mind."

James straightened himself. He tried to give the other man a knowing look. "I have been about a good deal," he said. "You need not be afraid of corrupting *me*."

Doctor Gordon laughed. "Well, I shall not try," he said. "At least, I shall not mean to corrupt you. I am a pessimist, but you are so young that you ought not to be influenced by that. Lord, only think what may be before you. You don't know. I am so far along that I know as far as I am concerned. I did not know but you had been brought up to think that whatever the Lord made was good, and that in saying that this red, gluey New Jersey soil was darned bad, I was swearing the worst way. I don't want to have millstones and that sort of thing about my neck. I was quite up in the Scriptures at one time."

"You need not be afraid," said James with dignity; "I think the soil darned bad myself." He hesitated a little over the darned, but once it was out, he felt proud of it.

"Yes, it is," said Doctor Gordon, "and if the Lord made it, he did not altogether succeed, and I see no earthly way of tracing the New Jersey soil back to original sin and the Garden of Eden."

"That's so," said James.

Doctor Gordon's face grew sober, his jocular mood for the time had vanished. He was his true self. "Did it ever occur to you that disease was the devil?" he asked abruptly. "That is, that all these infernal microbes that burrow in the human system to its disease and death, were his veritable imps at work?"

James shook his head, and looked curiously at his companion's face with its gloomy corrugations.

"Well, it has to me," said the doctor, "and let me ask you one thing. You have been brought up to believe that the devil's particular residence was hell, haven't you?"

James replied in a bewildered fashion that he had.

"Well," said Doctor Gordon, "if the devil lives here, as he must live, when there's such failures in the way of soil, and such climates, and such fiendish diseases, and crimes, why, this is hell."

James stared at him.

Doctor Gordon nodded half-gloomily, half-whimsically. "It's so," he said. "We call it earth; but it's hell."

James said nothing. The doctor's gloomy theology was too much for him. Besides, he was not quite sure that the elder man was not chaffing him.

"Well," said Doctor Gordon presently, "hell it is, but there are compensations, such as apple-jack, and now and then there's something doing that amuses one even here. I am going to take you to something that enlivens hell this afternoon, if somebody doesn't send a call. I am trying to get my work done this morning, the worst of it, so as to have an hour this afternoon."

The two returned a little after twelve, and found luncheon waiting for them. Mrs. Ewing took her place at the table, and James thought that she did not look quite so ill as she had done the evening before. She talked more, and ate with some appetite. Doctor Gordon's face lightened, not with the false gayety which James had seen, but he really looked quite happy, and spoke affectionately to his sister.

"What do you think, Tom," said she, "has come over Clemency? I don't know when there has been a morning that she has not gone for a tramp, rain or shine, but she has not stirred out today. She says she feels quite well, but I don't know."

"Oh, Clemency is all right," said Doctor Gordon, but his face darkened again. As for Clemency, she bent over her plate and looked sulkier than ever. She fairly pouted.

"She can go out this afternoon," said Mrs. Ewing. "It looks as if it were going to clear off."

"No, I don't want to go," said Clemency. "I am all out of the humor of it." She spoke with an air of animosity, as if somebody were to blame, but when she saw Mrs. Ewing's anxious eyes she smiled. "I would much prefer staying with you, dear," she said, "and finish Annie's Christmas present." She spoke with such an affectionate air, that James looked admiringly at her. She seemed a fellow-worshipper. He thought that he, too, would much prefer staying with Mrs. Ewing than going with Doctor Gordon on the mysterious outing which he had planned.

However, directly after luncheon Gordon led James out into the stable and called Aaron. "Are they ready, Aaron?" inquired the doctor.

Aaron grinned, opened a rude closet, and produced a number of objects, which James recognized at once as dummy pigeons. So Doctor Gordon was to take him to a pigeon-shooting match. James felt a little disgusted. He had, in fact, taken part in that sport with considerable gusto himself, but, just now, he being fairly launched, as it were, upon the serious things of life, took it somewhat in dudgeon that Doctor Gordon should think to amuse him with such frivolities. But to his amazement the elder man's face was all a-quiver with mirth and fairly eager. "Show the pigeons to Doctor Elliot, Aaron," said Doctor Gordon. James took one of the rude disks called pigeons from the hand of Aaron with indifference, then he started and stared at Doctor Gordon, who laughed like a boy, fairly doubling himself with merriment. Aaron did not laugh, he chewed on, but his eyes danced.

"Why, they are—" stammered James.

"Just so, young man," replied Doctor Gordon. "They are wood. Aaron made them on a lathe, and not a soul can tell them from the clay pigeons unless they handle them. Now you are going to see some fun. Jim Goodman, who is the meanest skunk in town, has cheated every mother's son of us first and last, and this afternoon he is going to shoot against Albert Dodd, and he's going to get his finish! Dodd knows about it. He'll have clay pigeons all right. Goodman has put up quite a sum of money, and he stands fair to lose for once in his life."

"Come on, Aaron, put the bay mare in the buggy. We'll drive down to the field. We haven't got much time to spare."

Aaron backed the mare out of her stall and hitched her to the mud-bespattered buggy, and the two men drove off with the wooden pigeons under the seat. They had not far to go, to a large field intersected with various footpaths and with, a large bare space, which evidently served as a football gridiron. "This field is used like town property," explained the doctor, "but the funny part of it is, it belongs to an old woman who is, perhaps, the richest person in Alton, and asks such a price for the land that nobody can buy it, and it has never occurred to her to keep off trespassers. So everybody trespasses, and she pays the taxes, and we are all satisfied, especially as there are plenty of better building sites in Alton to be bought for less money. That old woman bites her nose off every day, and never knows it."

On this barren expanse, intersected with the narrow footpaths, covered between with the no color of last year's dry weeds and grass, were assembled some half dozen men and boys. They rushed up as the doctor's buggy came alongside. "Got 'em?" they cried eagerly. Doctor Gordon fumbled under the seat and drew out the batch of wooden pigeons, which one young fellow, who seemed to be master of ceremonies, grasped and rushed off with to the queer-looking machine erected in the centre of the football clearing, for the purpose of making them take wing. The others went with him. Doctor Gordon got out of his buggy, accompanied by James, and they, too, joined the little group. "Got the others?" asked Gordon in a half whisper.

"Yes, you bet. We've got the others all right," said the young fellow, and everybody laughed.

Men and boys began to gather until the field was half filled with them. They all wore grinning countenances. "For Heaven's sake, boys, don't act as if it were so awful funny, or you'll spoil the whole thing," said the young fellow who had come for the pigeons.

Only one face was entirely sober, even severe, as with resolve, and that was the face of a small, mean-looking man between forty and fifty. He carried a gun, and looked at once important and greedy. "That's Jim Goodman," whispered Doctor Gordon to James, "and he's a crack shot, too. Albert isn't as sure, though he's pretty good, too."

James began to catch the spirit of it himself. He felt at once disgusted and uneasy about the doctor, but as for himself he was only a young man, after all, and sport was still sweet to his soul. He shouted with the rest when the first pigeon was launched into the air, and Albert Dodd, a tall, serious young man, fired. He hit the bird, which at once flew into fragments, as a clay pigeon properly should.

Georgie K. came up and joined them. He was evidently not in the secret, for he looked intensely puzzled when Jim Goodman, who had next shot, hit his bird fairly, but it only hopped about and descended unbroken. "What the deuce!" he said.

"Hush up, Georgie K.," said Doctor Gordon. The other man turned and looked at him keenly, but the doctor's imperturbable, smiling face was on the sport. Georgie K.'s great pink face grew grave. Every time Albert Dodd fired the pigeons dropped in pieces, every time Jim Goodman fired they hopped as if they were alive. Jim Goodman swore audibly. He looked to his cartridges. The whole field was in an uproar of mirth. The gunshots were hardly audible for the yells and wild halloos of merriment. The match at last was finished. Jim Goodman's last pigeon hopped, and he was upon it in a rage. He took it up and examined it. It was riddled with shot. He felt it, weighed it. Then his face grew fairly black. From being only mean, he looked murderous. He was losing money, and money was the closest thing to his soul. He looked around at the yelling throng, one man at bay, and he achieved a certain dignity, even in the midst of absurdity.

"This darned pigeon is wood," said he. "They are all wood, all I have shot. This is a put-up job! It ain't fair." He turned to the young fellow who had taken the pigeons, and who acted as referee.

"See here, John," he said, "you ain't going to see me done this way, be you? You know it ain't a fair deal. Albert Dodd's shot clay pigeons, and I've shot wood. It ain't fair."

"No, it ain't fair," admitted the young fellow reluctantly, with a side glance at Doctor Gordon. Gordon made a movement, but Georgie K. was ahead of him. James saw a roll of bills pass from his hands to Jim Goodman's. Gordon came up to Georgie K.

"See here!" he said.

"Well," replied Georgie K., without turning his head.

"Georgie K."

"I can't stop. Excuse me, Doc." Georgie K. jumped into a light wagon on that side of the field, and was gone with a swift bounce over the hollow which separated it from the road. Doctor Gordon hurried back to his own buggy, with James following, got in and took the road after Georgie K. "He mustn't pay that money," said Gordon. James said nothing.

"I never thought of such a thing as that," said Doctor Gordon, driving furiously, but they did not catch up with Georgie K. until they reached the Evarts House, and he was out of his wagon.

Doctor Gordon approached him, pocketbook in hand. "See here, Georgie K.," he said, "I owe you a hundred."

"Owe me nothing," said Georgie K. It had seemed impossible for his great pink face to look angry and contemptuous, but it did. "I don't set up for much," said he, "but I must say I like a square deal."

"Good Lord! so do I," said Gordon. "Here, take this money. I had Aaron make those darned wooden pigeons. Jim Goodman has skinned enough young chaps here to deserve the taste of a skin himself."

"He ain't skinned you."

"Hasn't he? He owes me for two wives' last sicknesses, to say nothing of himself and children, and he's living with his third, and I shall have to doctor her for nothing or let her die. But that wasn't what I did it for."

Georgie K. turned upon him. "What on earth did you do it for, Doc?" said he.

"Because I felt the way you have felt yourself."

"When?"

"When the woman that made those wax-flowers, and loved that little stuffed bird in there, died."

Georgie K.'s face paled. "What's the matter, Doc?"

"Nothing, I tell you."

"What?"

"Nothing. Who said there was anything? I had to have my little joke. I tell you, Georgie K., I've *got* to have my little joke, just as I've got to have my game of euchre with you and my glass of apple-jack; a man can't be driven too far. I meant to make it right with him. He's a mean little cuss, but I am not mean. I intended to spend a hundred on my joke, and you got ahead of me. For God's sake, take the money, Georgie K."

Georgie K., still with a white, shocked, inquiring face, extended his hand and took the roll of bills which the doctor gave him.

"Come in and take something," said he, and Doctor Gordon and James accepted. They went again into the state parlor on whose shelf were the wax-flowers and the stuffed canary, and they partook of apple-jack.

Then Doctor Gordon and James took leave. Georgie K. gave Gordon a hearty shake of the hand when he got into the buggy. Gordon looked at James again with his gloomy face, as he took up the lines. "Failed in the race again," he said. "Now we've got to hustle, for I have eight calls to make before dinner, and it's late. I ought to change horses, but there isn't time."

CHAPTER IV

The weeks went on, and James led the same life with practically no variation. The sense of a mystery or mysteries about the house never left him, and it irritated him. He was not curious; he did not in the least care to know in what the mystery consisted, but the fact of concealment itself was obnoxious to him. As for himself, he never concealed anything, and when it came to mystery, he had a vague idea of something shameful, if not criminal. Doctor Gordon's incomprehensible changes of mood, of almost more than mood, of character even, disturbed him. Why a man should be one hour a country buffoon, the next an absorbed gentleman, he could not understand. And he could not understand also why Clemency had never left the house since he had met her on the day of his arrival. She evidently was herself angry and sulky at being housed, but she did not attempt to resist, and whenever Mrs. Ewing expressed anxiety about her health, she laughed it off, and made some excuse, such as the badness of the roads, or some Christmas work which she was anxious to finish. However, at last Mrs. Ewing's concern grew so evident that Doctor Gordon at dinner one day gave what seemed a plausible reason for Clemency remaining indoors. "If you will have it, Clara," he said, "Clemency has a slight pain in her side, and pleurisy and pneumonia are all about, and I told her that she had better take no chances, and the weather has been raw."

Mrs. Ewing turned quite white. "Oh, Tom," she murmured, "why didn't you tell me?"

"I did not tell you, Clara dear, because you would immediately have had the child in a galloping consumption, and it is really nothing at all. I only want to be on the safe side."

"It is a very little pain, mother dear," said Clemency. When Clemency spoke to Mrs. Ewing, her voice had a singing quality. At such times, although the young man's very soul was possessed of the mother, he could not help viewing the daughter with favor. But he was puzzled about the pleurisy. The girl seemed to him entirely well, although she was losing a little of her warm color from staying indoors. Still, after all, a pain is as invisible as a spirit. Her friend, Annie Lipton, spent a few days with her, and then James saw very little of Clemency. The two girls sat together in Clemency's room, and only the Lord of innocence and ignorance knew what they talked about. They talked a great deal. James, whenever he was in the house, was conscious of the distant murmur of their sweet young voices, although he could not distinguish a word. Annie Lipton was a prettier girl than Clemency, though without her personal charm. Her beauty seemed to abash her, and make her indignant. She was a girl who should have been a nun, and viewed love and lovers from behind iron bars. She treated James with exceeding coolness.

"Annie Lipton is an anomaly," Doctor Gordon remarked once over his after-dinner pipe, when they sat in the study listening to the feminine murmur on the other side of the wall. It sounded like the gentle ripple of a summer sea.

"Why?" returned James.

"She defies her sex," replied Doctor Gordon, "and still there is nothing mannish about her. She is a woman angry and ashamed at her womanhood. If she ever marries, it will be at the cost of a terrible mental struggle. There are women-haters among men, and there are a very few—so few as to rank with albinos and white blackbirds in scarcity—man-haters among women. Annie is a man-hater."

"She is very pretty, too," said James.

"If you attempt the conquest, I'll warn you there will be scaling ladders and all the ancient paraphernalia of siege needed," said Doctor Gordon laughingly. James colored.

"It may be that I am a woman-hater," he replied, and looked very young. Doctor Gordon again laughed.

A little later they went to Georgie K.'s. They went nearly every evening while Annie Lipton was with Clemency. After she had left they did not go so often. "It is pretty dull for Clemency," Doctor Gordon would say, and they would remain at home and play whist with the two ladies. James began to be quite sure that Doctor Gordon's visits to Georgie K.'s were mostly made when Mrs. Ewing looked worse than usual and did not eat her dinner. James became convinced in his own mind that Mrs. Ewing was not well, although he never dared broach the subject again to the doctor, and although it made no difference whatever in his own attitude toward her. As well might he have turned his back upon the Venus, because of some slight abrasion which her beautiful body had received from the ages.

But one day, having come in unexpectedly alone, he found her on the divan in the living-room, evidently weeping, and his heart went out to her. He flung himself down on his knees beside her.

"Oh, what is it? What is the matter?" he whispered.

Her whole body was writhing. She uncovered her eyes and looked at him pitifully, and yet with a certain dignity. Those beautiful eyes, brimming with tears, were not reddened, and their gaze was steady. "If I tell you, will you keep my secret?" she whispered back, "or, rather, it is not a secret since Doctor Gordon knows it. I wish he did not, but will you keep your knowledge from him?"

"I promise you I will," said James fervently.

"I am terribly ill," said Mrs. Ewing simply. "I suffer at times tortures. Don't ask me what the matter is. It is too dreadful, and although I have no reason to feel so, it seems to me ignominious. I am ashamed of being so ill. I feel disgraced by it, wicked." She covered her face again and sobbed.

"Don't, don't," said James, out of his senses completely. "Don't, I can't bear it. I love you so. Don't! I will cure you."

"You cannot. Doctor Gordon does not admit that my case is hopeless, but he gives no hope, and you must have noticed how he suffers when he sees me suffer. He runs away from me because he can do nothing to help me. That is the worst of it all. I could bear the pain for myself, but for the others, too! Oh, I wish there was some little back door of life out of which one could slip, and no blame to anybody, in a case like this. But there is nothing but the horrible front door, which means such agony to everybody who is left, as well as the one that goes." Mrs. Ewing had completely lost control of herself. She sobbed again and moaned.

James covered one of her cold hands with kisses. "Don't, don't," he begged. "Don't, I love you."

Suddenly Mrs. Ewing came to the comprehension of what he said. She looked at his bent head—James had a curly head like a boy's—and a strange look came into her eyes, as if she were regarding him across an immeasurable gulf. Nobody had ever seemed quite so far away in the world as this boy with his cry of love to the woman old enough to be his mother. It was not the fact of her superior age alone, it was her disease, it was her sense of being done forever with anything like this that gave her, as it were, a view of earth from outside, and yet she had a sense of comfort. James was even weeping. She felt his tears on her hand. It did her good that anybody could love her so little as to be able to stay by and see her suffer, and weep for her, and not rush forth in a rage of misery like

Thomas Gordon. In a second, however, she had command of herself. She drew her hand away. "Doctor Elliot," she said, "you forget yourself."

"No, no, I don't," protested James. "It is not as if I—I were thinking of you in that way. I am not. I know you could not possibly think of me as a girl might. It is only because I love you. I have never seen anybody like you."

"You must put me out of your head," said Mrs. Ewing. "I am old enough to be your mother; I am ill unto death. You must not love me in any way."

"I cannot help it"

Mrs. Ewing hesitated. "I have a mind to tell you something," she said in a low voice. "Can I rely upon you?"

"I would die before I told, if you said I was not to," cried James.

"It might almost come to that," said the woman gravely. "A very serious matter is involved, otherwise there would not be this secrecy. I cannot tell you what the matter is, but I can tell you something which will cure you of loving me."

"I don't want to be cured," protested James, "and I have told you it is a love like worship, it is not—"

Mrs. Ewing interrupted him. "The worship of a young man is not to be trusted," she said. "I cannot have you made to suffer. I will tell you, but, remember, if you betray me you will do awful harm. Neither the doctor nor Clemency even must know that I tell you. The doctor knows, of course, the secret; Clemency does not know, and must never know. It would be the undoing of all of us, the terrible undoing, if this were to get out, but I will tell you. You are a good boy, and you shall be spared needless pain. Listen." She leaned forward and whispered close to his ear. James started back, and stared at her as white as death. Mrs. Ewing smiled. "It hurts a little, I know," she said, "but better this now than worse later. You are foolish to feel so about me; you were at a disadvantage in coming here. It is only right that you should know. Now never speak to me again about this. Think of me as your friend, and your friend who is in very great suffering and pain, and have sympathy for me, if you can, but not so much sympathy that you too will suffer. I want sympathy, but not agony like poor Tom's. That makes it harder for me."

"Does she know?" asked James, half-gasping.

"You mean does Clemency know I am ill?"

"Yes."

"She knows I am ill. She does not know how terrible it is. You must help me to keep it from her. I almost never give way when she is present. I knew she was taking a nap this afternoon, and the pain was so awful. It is better now. I think I will go to my room and lie down for a while." Mrs. Ewing rose, and extended her hand to James. "I have forgotten already what you told me," she said.

"I can never forget!"

"You must, or you must go away from here."

"I can never forget, but it shall be a thing of the past," said James.

"That is right," Mrs. Ewing said with a maternal air. "It will only take a little effort. You will see."

She went out of the room with a flounce of red draperies, and left James. He sat down beside a window and stared out blankly. The thought came to him, how many avowals of love and deathless devotion such a woman must have listened to. Her manner of receiving his made him think that there had been many. "It is quite proper," he thought to himself. "A woman like that is born to be worshiped." Then he thought of what she had told him, and a sort of rage filled his heart. He recognized the fact that she had been right in her estimation of the worship of a young man. He is always trying to turn his idol into clay.

The door opened and Clemency entered, but he did not notice it. She came and sat down in front of him, and looked angrily at him, then for the first time he saw her. He rose. "I beg your pardon, I did not hear you come in," he said.

"Sit down again," said Clemency pettishly. "Don't be silly. I am used to having young men not see anybody but my mother when she comes into a room, and it is quite right, too. I don't think there ever was a woman so beautiful as she, do you?"

"No, I don't," replied James.

Clemency eyed him keenly. Then she blushed at the surmise which came to her, and James also blushed at the knowledge of the surmise. "You can't be much older than I am. I am twenty-three," said Clemency after a while. Then the red suffused her very throat.

"I am twenty-three, too," said James. Then he added bluntly, for he began to be angry, "A man can think a woman the most beautiful he ever saw without—"

"Oh, I didn't think you were such a fool," said Clemency; then she added, in a meek and shamed voice, "I should have been awfully disgusted with you if you had not thought my mother the most beautiful woman you ever saw, and I am used to men not seeing me. I don't want them to. I think I feel something as Annie Lipton does about men. She says she feels as if she wanted to kill every man who looks at her as if he loved her. I think I should, too."

"Miss Lipton has a great many admirers," remarked James by way of changing the subject.

"Oh, yes, every young man for miles around, ever since she was grown up. She doesn't like any of them." Clemency looked at James with sudden concern. "I am going to tell you something," she said, "even if it is rather betraying confidence. I think I ought to. Annie told me she had taken a great dislike to you, from the very first moment she saw you, so it would be no use—"

"I am sorry," replied James stiffly, "but as I had no particular feeling for her, except admiration of her beauty, it makes no especial difference."

"I thought, of course, you would fall in love with her," said Clemency. Then she added, with most inexplicable inverted jealousy, "You must have very poor taste, or you would. You are the first one."

"Some one has to be first," James said, laughing.

"I don't know but I was horrid to tell you what I did," said Clemency, looking at him doubtfully.

"I don't think it as horrid for a girl to assume that every man is in love with her friend as it would be if she assumed something else," said James. He knew that his speech was ungallant; but it seemed to him that this girl fairly challenged him to rudeness. But she looked at him innocently.

"Oh, no, I never should think that," said she. "Being with two women so very beautiful as my mother and Annie so much makes me quite sure that nobody is thinking of me. It is only sometimes that I feel a little like a piece of furniture, only chairs can't walk into rooms." She ended with a girlish laugh. Then her face suddenly sobered. "Doctor Elliot, I want you to tell me something," said she. "Uncle Tom wouldn't if I asked him, and I don't dare ask him anyway. Do you think mother is very well?"

James hesitated. "You ought to tell me," Clemency said imperatively.

"I have thought sometimes that she did not look quite well," said James.

"What do you think the matter is?"

"It may be indigestion."

"Do you think it is?"

"I don't know. Doctor Gordon has told me nothing, and Mrs. Ewing has told me nothing."

"I thought doctors could tell from a person's looks."

"Not always."

"Doctors aren't much good anyhow," said Clemency. "I don't care if you are one, and Uncle Tom is one. I notice people die just the same. So you think it is indigestion? Well, it may be. Mother doesn't have much appetite."

"Yes, I have noticed that," said James.

"Then there is something else I want to ask you," said Clemency. "I have a right to know if you know. What does Uncle Tom make me stay in the house so for?"

"I don't know," replied James, looking honestly at her.

"Don't you, honest? Hasn't he told you?"

"No."

"Of course, I know the first of it came from my meeting that man the day you came here, but it does seem such utter nonsense that I have to stay housed this way. I never met a man that frightened me before, and it is not likely that I shall again. It does not stand to reason that that man is hanging around here waiting to intercept me again. It is nonsense, but Uncle Tom won't let me stir out. He has even ordered me to keep away from the windows, and be sure that the curtains are drawn at night. I don't know what the matter is. I can't say a word about it to mother, she is so nervous. I have to pretend that I like to stay in the house, and some days I really think I am going mad for fresh air. Uncle Tom won't even let me go driving with him. So you don't know anything about it?"

"Nothing whatever."

"Well, I can't stand it much longer," said Clemency with an obstinate look. "As for the pain in my side, that's an awful lie; I haven't the ghost of a pain. I can't stand it much longer. Here's Uncle Tom. You are not going to tell him I said anything about it?"

"Of course, I am not," answered James. He began to feel that he was entangled in a web of secrecy, and his feeling of irritation increased. He would have gotten out of it and spent Christmas at his own home, but Doctor Gordon had an unusual number of patients suffering from grippe, and pneumonia was almost epidemic, and he felt that he should not leave. It was the second week of the new year when James, returning from a call at a near-by patient, whither he had walked, found Mrs. Ewing in the greatest distress. It was ten o'clock at night, and she was pacing the living-room. Immediately when he entered she ran to him. "Oh," she gasped, "Clemency, Clemency!"

"Why, what is it?" asked James. Clemency had not been at the dinner-table, but he had supposed her sulking, as she had been doing of late, and that she had taken advantage of Doctor Gordon's absence at a distant patient's to remain away from the table.

"She begged so hard to go out, and said the pain was quite well," gasped Mrs. Ewing, "that I said she might go and see Annie, and here it is ten o'clock at night, and Tom has gone to Grover's Corner, and may not be home until morning, and Aaron is with him, and I had no one to send. I thought I would not say anything to you. I thought every minute she would come in, and Emma has walked half a mile looking for her, and I am horribly worried."

"I will go directly and look for her," said James. "I will put the bay in the light buggy, and drive to Westover. Don't worry. I'll bring her back in half an hour."

"The bay is so lame she can't travel, I heard Tom say this morning," said Mrs. Ewing.

"Then I'll take the gray."

"She balks, you know."

James laughed. "Oh, I'll risk the balking," he said.

He hurried out to the stable and put the gray in the buggy. It was a very short time before James was on the road, and the gray went as well as could be desired, but just before she reached Westover she stopped short, and James might as well have tried to move a mountain as that animal with her legs planted at four angles of relentless obstinacy.

CHAPTER V

James had considerable experience with, horses. He knew at once that it was probably a hopeless undertaking to change the mare's mind, or rather her obstinacy. However, he tried the usual methods, touching with the whip, getting out and attempting to lead, but they were all, as he had supposed from the first, in vain. A terrible sense of being up against fate itself seized him: an animal's will unreasoning, unrelenting, bears, in fact, the aspect of fate itself. It is at once sensate and insensate. James thought of Clemency, and decided to waste no more time.

The gray mare was near enough to a tree to tie her, and he tied her and set out on foot. It was a very dark night, cloudy and chilly and threatening snow. He walked on, as it were, through softly enveloping shadows, which seemed to his excited fancy to be coming forward to meet him. He began to be very much alarmed. He had wasted most of his young sentiment upon Clemency's mother, but, after all, he suddenly discovered that he had a feeling for the girl herself. He thought that it was only the natural anxiety of any man of honor for the safety of a helpless young girl out alone at night, and beset by possible dangers, but he realized himself in a panic. His plan was of course to go directly to Annie Lipton's home, some two miles farther on, then it occurred to him that Clemency must inevitably have left there. If she were lying dead or injured on the road, how in the world was he to see? He felt in his pocket for matches, and found just one. He lit that and peered around. While it burned he saw nothing except the frozen road with its desolate borders of woods and brush, a fit scene for countless tragedies. When the match burned out he thought of something else. Supposing that Clemency were lying half-dead anywhere near the road, how was she to know that a friend was near? Immediately he began to whistle. Whistling was a trick of his, and he had a remarkably sweet, clear pipe. He knew that Clemency, if she were to hear his whistle, would know who was near. He whistled "Way down upon the Suwannee River" through, then he began on the "Flower Song" from Faust, walking all the time quite rapidly but with alert ears. He was half through the "Flower Song" when he stopped short. He thought he heard something. He listened, and did hear quite distinctly an exceedingly soft little voice, which might have been the voice of shadows—"Is that you?"

"Clemency," he cried out, and rushed toward the wood, and directly the girl was clinging to him. She was panting with sobs, but she kept her voice down to a whisper.

"Speak low, speak low," she said in his ear. "I don't know where he is. Oh, speak low." She clung to him with almost a spasmodic grip of her slender arms. "If you had been ten minutes longer I think I should have died," she whispered. "Don't make a sound. I don't know where he is."

"Yes, that same dreadful man. Uncle Tom was right. I stayed too long at Annie's. It was almost dark when I left there. She persuaded me to stay to dinner. They had turkey. I was about half a mile below here when he, the man, came out of the woods, just as he did before. I heard him, and I knew. I did not look around. I ran, and I heard his footsteps behind me. The darkness seemed to shut down all at once. I knew he could catch me, and remembered what I had heard about wild animals when they were hunted. I had gone a little past here, running just as softly as I could, when I turned right into the woods, and ran back. Then I lay right down in the underbrush and kept still. I heard him run past. Then I heard him come back. He came into the woods. I expected every minute he would step on me, but I kept still. Finally I heard him go away, but I have not dared to stir since! I made up my mind I would keep still until I heard a team pass. It did seem to me one must pass, and one would have at any other time, but it has been hours I have been lying there. Then I heard your whistle. I was almost afraid to speak then. Don't speak above a whisper now. Did you come on foot?"

"I had the gray mare, and she balked about half a mile from here. You are sure you are not hurt?"

"No, only I am trying hard not to faint. Let us walk on very fast, but step softly, and don't talk."

James put his arm around the girl and half carried her. She continued to draw short, panting breaths, which she tried to subdue. They reached the place where the gray mare loomed faintly out of the gloom with the dark mass of the buggy behind her.

"Let us get in," whispered Clemency. "Quick!"

"I am afraid she won't budge."

"Yes, she will for me. She has a tender mouth, that is why she balks. You must have pulled too hard on the lines. Sometimes I have made her go when even Uncle Tom couldn't."

Clemency ran around to the gray's head and patted her, and

James untied her. Then the girl got into the buggy and took the reins, and James followed. He was almost jostled out, the mare started with such impetus. They made the distance home almost on a run.

"Oh, I am so glad," panted Clemency. "You see I can seem to feel her mouth when I hold the lines, and she knows. Was poor mother worried?"

"A little."

"I know she was almost crazy."

"She will be all right when she sees you safe," said James.

"Is Uncle Tom home yet? No, of course I know he isn't, or he would have come instead of you. Oh, dear, I know he will scold me. I shall have to tell him, but I mustn't tell mother about the man. What shall I tell her? It is dreadful to have to lie, but sometimes one would rather run the risk of fire and brimstone for one's self than have anybody else hurt. If I tell mother she will have one of her dreadful nervous attacks. I can't tell her. What shall I tell her, Doctor Elliot?"

"I think the simplest thing will be to say that Miss Lipton persuaded you to stay to supper, and so you were late, and I overtook you," said James.

"Mother will never believe that I stayed so long as that," said Clemency. "I shall have to lie more than that. I don't know exactly what to say. I could have Charlie Horton come in to play whist, and be taking me home in his buggy. He always drives, and you could meet me on the road."

"Yes, you could do that."

"It is a very complicated lie," said Clemency, "but I don't know that a complicated lie is any worse than a simple one. I think I shall have to lie the complicated one. You need not say anything, you know. You can take the mare to the stable, and I will run in and get the lie all told before you come. You won't lie, will you?"

James could not help laughing. "No, I don't see any need of it," he replied.

"It is rather awful for you to have to live with people who have to lie so," remarked Clemency, "but I don't see how it can be helped. If you had seen my mother in one of her nervous attacks once, you would never want to see her again. There is only one thing, I do feel very weak still, and I am afraid I shall look pale. Hold the lines a minute. Don't pull on them at all. Let them lie on your knees."

"What are you doing?" asked James when he had complied.

"Doing? I am pinching my cheeks almost black and blue, so mother won't notice. I don't talk scared now, do I?"

"Not very."

"Well, I think I can manage that. I think I can manage my voice. I am all over being faint. Oh, I will tell you what I will do. You haven't got your medicine-case with you, have you?"

"No, I started so hurriedly."

"Well, I will go in the office way. I know where Uncle Tom keeps brandy, and I will be so chilled that I'll have to take a little before mother sees me. That will make me all right. I wouldn't take it for myself, but I will for her."

"And you are chilled, all right," said James.

"Yes, I think I am," said Clemency. "I did not think of it, but I guess it was cold there in the woods keeping still so long." Indeed, the girl was shaking from head to foot, both with cold and nervous terror. "It was awful," she said in a little whisper.

James felt the girl shaking from head to foot. Suddenly a great tenderness for the poor, little hunted thing came over him. He put his arm around her. "Poor little soul," he said. "It must have been terrible for you lying out there in the cold and dark and not knowing—"

Clemency shrank into his embrace as a hurt child might have done. "It was perfectly terrible," she said, with a little sob. "I didn't know but he might come back any minute and find me."

"It is all over now," James said soothingly.

"Yes, for the time," Clemency replied with a little note of despair in her voice, "but there is something about it all that I don't understand. Only think how long I have had to stay in the house, and he must have been on the watch. I don't know when it is ever going to end."

"I think that I will end it tomorrow," said James with fierce resolution.

"You? How?"

"I am going to put a stop to this. If an innocent girl can't step out of the house for weeks at a time without being hounded this way, it is high time something was done. I am going to get a posse of men and scour the country for the scoundrel."

"Oh, will you do that?"

"Yes, I will. It is high time somebody did something."

"You saw him. You know just how he looks?"

"I could tell him from a thousand."

Clemency drew a long breath. "Well," she said doubtfully, "if you can, but—"

"But what?"

"Nothing, only somehow I doubt if Uncle Tom will think it advisable. There must be some mystery about all this or Uncle Tom himself would have done that very thing at first. I don't understand it. But I don't believe Uncle Tom will consent to your hunting for the man. I think for some reason he wants it kept secret." Suddenly, Clemency gave a passionate little outcry. "Oh, how I do hate secrets!" she said. "How I have always hated them! I want everything right out, and here I seem to be in a perfect snarl of secrets! I wonder how long I shall have to stay in the house."

"Perhaps you are wrong, and your uncle will take measures now this has happened for the second time," said James.

"No, he won't," replied the girl hopelessly. "I am almost sure that he will not."

Clemency was right. After she had made her entry and told her little lie successfully, and explained that she had taken some brandy because she was chilled, and Mrs. Ewing had gently scolded her for staying so late, and kissed and embraced her, and gotten back her own composure, Doctor Gordon arrived, and James, who had waited for him in the study, told him the story in whispers. "Now I think you had better let me get a posse of men and scour the country tomorrow," he concluded. "It seems to me that this thing has gone far enough."

Doctor Gordon sat huddled up before him in an arm-chair. He had not even taken off his overcoat, which was white with snow. The storm had begun. "It will be easy to track him on account of the snow," added James.

"Tracking is not necessary," replied Gordon, with his haggard face fixed upon James. "I know exactly where the man is, and have known from the first."

"Then—" began James.

"You don't know what you are talking about," Gordon said gloomily. "I would have that fiend arrested tomorrow. I would have him hung from the nearest tree if I had my way, but I can do absolutely nothing."

"Nothing?"

"No, I can do nothing, except what I have been doing, so far in vain, it seems, to try to tire him out. I traded too much on his impatience, it seemed. I did not think he would have held out so long."

"You mean you will have to keep that poor little thing shut up the way you have been doing?"

"I see no other way. God knows I have tried to think of another, day and night."

"I don't see why you or I could not take her out sometimes when we visit patients anyway," said James in a bewildered fashion.

"You don't understand," replied Doctor Gordon irritably. "The main point is: the girl must not be even seen by that man. That is the trouble. Driving, she might be perfectly safe; in fact, in one way she is safe anyhow. She is not in any danger of bodily harm, as you may think, but I don't want her seen."

"Why not let me take her out sometimes of an evening then?" said James, more and more mystified. "If she wore a veil, and went out driving in the evening, I can't see how anybody could get a glimpse of her."

"You don't understand that we have to deal with a very devil incarnate," said Doctor Gordon wearily. "He will be on the watch for just that very manoeuvre. However, perhaps we may be able to manage that; I will see."

"She will be ill if she remains in the house so closely," said James, "especially a girl like her, who has been accustomed to lead such an outdoor life. In fact, I don't think she does look very well now. It is telling on her."

"Yes, I think it is," agreed Doctor Gordon gloomily, "but again, I say, I see no other way out of it. However, perhaps you or I can take her out sometimes of an evening. I suppose it had better be you, on some accounts. I will see. Well, I will take off my coat and get something to eat. I suppose Clara and Clemency have gone to bed."

"They went hours ago," replied James. It was, in fact, two in the morning. James followed the doctor, haggard and weary, into the kitchen, where, according to custom at such times, some dinner had been left to keep warm on the range. "I'll sit down here," said Doctor Gordon. "It is warmer than in the dining-room, and I am chilled through. If you don't mind, Elliot, I wish you would get me a bottle of apple-jack from the dining-room. I must have something to hearten me up, or I shall go by the board, and I don't know what will become of her—of them."

James sat and waited while the doctor ate and drank. When he had finished he looked a little less haggard. He stretched himself before the warm glow from the range and laughed. "Now I feel my fighting blood is up again," he said. "After all, if there is anything in the Good Book, the wicked shall not always triumph, and I may win out. I shall do my best anyhow. But I confess you took the wind out of me with what you told me when I came in. I am glad Clara does not know. Poor little Clemency having to pave her way with lies, but it would kill Clara. Oh, God, it does seem as if I had enough before. Take my advice, young man, and try to think more of yourself than anybody else in the world. Don't let your heart go out to anybody. Just as sure as you do, the door of the worst torture-chamber in creation swings open. The minute you become vulnerable through love, you haven't a strong place in your whole armor."

"What a doctrine!" observed James.

"I know it, but I have taken a fancy to you, boy; and hang it if I want you to suffer as I have to."

"But a man would not be a man at all if he did not think enough of somebody to suffer," said James, and now he was thinking of poor little Clemency, and how she had nestled up to him for protection.

"Maybe," said Doctor Gordon gloomily, "but sometimes I wonder whether it pays in the long run to be what you call a man. Sometimes I wish that I were a rock or a tree. I do tonight."

"You will feel better after you have had a little sleep," James said, as the two men rose.

Suddenly one of Doctor Gordon's inexplicable changes of mood came over him. He laughed. "If it were not so late we would go down to Georgie K.'s," said he. "I never felt more awake. Well, I guess it's too late. You must be dead tired yourself. I have not thanked you at all for your rescue of the girl. She would have been down with a serious illness if you had not gone, for she would have lain in that place being snowed over until somebody came."

"She was mighty clever to do what she did," said James.

"Yes, she is clever," returned Doctor Gordon. "She is a good girl, and it stings me to the very heart that she has to suffer such persecution. Well, 'all's well that ends well.' Did it ever occur to you that God made up to mankind for the horrors of creation, by stating that there would be an end to it some day? Good God, if this terrible world had to roll on to all eternity!" Doctor Gordon laughed again his unnatural laugh. "Fancy if you were awakened tonight by the last trump," he said. "How small everything would seem. Hang it, though, if I wouldn't try to have a hand at that man's finish before the angel of the Lord got his flaming sword at work."

James looked at him with terror.

"Don't mind me, boy," said Gordon. "I don't mean to blaspheme; but Job is not in it with me just now. You cannot imagine what I had to contend with before this melodramatic villain appeared on the stage. Sometimes I think this is the finish," Gordon's mouth contracted. He looked savage. James continued to stare at him. Gordon laid his hand on James's shoulder. "Thank the Lord for one thing," he said almost tenderly, "that he sent you here. Between us we will take care of poor little Clemency anyhow. Now go to bed, and go to sleep."

James obeyed as to the one, but he could not as to the other. He became, as the hours wore on, so nervous that he was half-inclined to take a sleeping powder. The room seemed full of flashes of lightning. He heard sounds which made him cold with horror. He was highly strung nervously, and was really in a state bordering upon hysteria. The mystery which surrounded him was the main cause. He was never himself before an unknown quantity. He had too much imagination. He made all sorts of surmises as to the stranger who was haunting Clemency. Starting with two known quantities, he might have accomplished something, but here he had only one: Clemency herself. He had a good head for algebra, but a man cannot work out a problem easily with only one known quantity. He began to wonder if the poor girl herself were sleeping. He realized a sort of protective tenderness for her, and indignation on her behalf. It did not occur to him as being love. Still the image of her wonderful mother dominated him. But his mind dwelt upon the girl. He thought of a piazza whose roof opened as he knew upon Clemency's room. He wondered if a man like that would stick at anything. Then he recalled what Doctor Gordon had said about Clemency's not being in any bodily danger, and again he speculated. The room began to grow pale with the late winter dawn. Familiar objects began to gain clearness of outline. There were two windows in James's room. They gave upon the piazza. Suddenly

James made a leap from his bed. He sprang to one of the windows. Flattened against it was the face of the man. But the face was so destitute of consciousness of him, that James doubted if he saw rightly. The wide eyes seemed to gaze upon him without seeing him, the mouth smiled as if at something within. The next moment James was sure that the face was not there. He drew on his trousers, thrust his feet into his shoes, and was out of his room and the house, and on the piazza. It was still snowing, but the dawn was overcoming the storm. The whole world was lit with dead white pallor like the face of a corpse. James rushed the length of the piazza. He looked at the walk leading to it. He thought he could distinguish footprints. He looked on the piazza, but the wind, being on the other side of the house, there was not enough snow there to make footprints visible. The snow on the walk was drifted. He looked at it closely, and made sure of deep marks. He stood for a moment undecided what to do. He disliked to arouse Doctor Gordon. He was afraid of awakening Mrs. Ewing, if he ventured into the upper part of the house. Then he thought of the man Aaron who slept in a room over the stable. He reëntered the house, locked the front door, went softly into the doctor's study, and out of the door which was near the stable. Then he made a hard snow-ball, and threw it at Aaron's window. The window opened directly, and Aaron's head appeared. James could see, even in the dim light, and presumably just awakened from sleep, the rotary motion of his jaws. He was probably not chewing anything, simply moving his mouth from force of habit. "Hullo!" said Aaron, "that you Doctor Gordon?"

"No, it is I," replied James. "Put on something as quick as you can, and come down here. Something is wrong."

Aaron's head disappeared. In an incredibly short space of time the stable door was unlocked and slid cautiously back, and Aaron stood there, huddled into his clothes. "What's up?" he asked.

"I don't know. Have you got a lantern in the stable?"

"Yep."

"Light it quick, then, and come along with me."

Aaron obeyed. "Anybody sick," he asked, coming alongside with the flashing lantern. He threw a cloth over it so as to prevent the rays shining into the house windows. "I don't want to frighten her," he said, and James knew that he meant Mrs. Ewing. "She's awful nervous," said Aaron. Then he said again, "What's up?"

"I saw a man's face looking into one of my windows," replied James.

Aaron gave a low whistle. "Somebody wanted the doc?" he inquired.

"No," replied James shortly, "it was not."

"Must have been."

"No, it was not."

"Must have been," repeated Aaron, chewing.

"I tell you it was not. I knew—" James stopped. He suddenly wondered how much he ought to tell the man, how much Doctor Gordon had told him.

Aaron chewed imperturbably, but a sly look came into his face. "I have eyes, and they see, and ears, and they hear," he said, after an odd Scriptural fashion, "but don't you tell me nothin', Doctor Elliot. Either I take what I get from the fountain-head, or I makes my own conclusions that I can't help. Don't you tell me nothin'. S'pose we look an' see ef there's footprints that show anythin'."

Aaron flashed the lantern, all the time carefully shading it from the house windows, over the walk which led to the front door and the piazza. James followed him. "Well," said Aaron, "there's been somebody here, but, with snow like this, it might have been a monkey or a rhinoceros or an alligator. You can't make nothin' of them tracks. But they do go out to the road, and turn toward Stanbridge."

"Suppose we—" began James. He was about to suggest following the prints, when he remembered Doctor Gordon's injunction to the contrary.

However, Aaron anticipated him. "Might as well leave the devil alone," said he. "It might have been the old one himself, for all we can tell by them tracks. You had better go back to bed, Doctor Elliot. You ain't got much on. It ain't near breakfast time yet. Better go back to bed."

And James thought such a course the wiser one himself. He went back to bed, but not to sleep. He kept his eyes fixed upon the windows. He was prepared at any instant, should the man reappear, to spring out. He felt almost murderous. "It has come to a pretty pass," he thought, "if that scoundrel, whoever he may be, is lurking around the house at night."

The daylight came slowly on account of the storm. When it did come, it was an opaque white daylight. James began to smell coffee and frying ham. He rose and dressed himself, and looked out of the window. It was like looking into a blurred mirror. He began to wonder if he could have been mistaken, if possibly that face had been simply a vision which had come from his overwrought brain. He wondered if he should tell Doctor Gordon, if it might not disturb him unnecessarily. He wondered if he should have enforced secrecy upon Aaron. He was still undecided when the Japanese gong sounded, and he went out to breakfast. Clemency was looking worn and ill. Somehow the sight of her piteous little face decided James. He thought how easily an athletic man could climb up one of those piazza posts, which was, moreover, encircled by a strong old vine which might almost serve as ladder. He made up his mind to tell Doctor Gordon, and he did tell him when they were out upon their rounds, tilting and sliding along the drifted country roads in an old sleigh. "I don't think I can be mistaken," he said when he had finished.

Doctor Gordon looked at him intently. "You are sure," he said. "You are a nervous subject for a man, and you had not slept, and you had this man very much on your mind, and there must have been some snow on the window which could produce an illusion. Be very sure, because this is serious."

James thought again of Clemency's little white face. "Yes," he said, "I am sure."

"You have no doubt at all?"

"None. The man had his face staring into the room. He did not seem to see me, but looked past me at the bed."

"He might easily have thought that room, being on the ground floor and accessible to night-calls, was mine," said Doctor Gordon, as if to himself.

"I thought how easily he could have climbed up one of the piazza posts to her room," said James.

The Doctor started. "Yes, that is so," he said. "He might have had two motives. That is so."

The next call was at a patient's who had a slight attack of grippe. Doctor Gordon left James there, saying that he would make another call and be back for him directly. James noticed how he urged the horses out of the drive at almost a run. He was back soon, and James having made up his prescription, went out and got into the sleigh. Doctor Gordon looked at him gloomily. "He is no longer where he has been staying," he said, and his face settled into a stern melancholy. That evening, although the storm continued, he suggested a visit to Georgie K.'s; and at supper time he insisted upon Clemency's occupying another room that night. "The wind is on your side of the house," he said, "and I am afraid you will take more cold." Clemency stared and pouted, then said, "All right, Uncle Tom!"

CHAPTER VI

Even the apple-jack and euchre at Georgie K.'s were not sufficient to entirely establish Doctor Gordon in his devil-may-care mood. Georgie K. kept looking at him with solicitation, which had something tender about it. "Don't you feel well, Doc?" he asked.

"Never felt better in my life," returned Gordon quickly. "Tonight I am feeling particularly good, because I really think I have evolved an utterly new theory of death and disease which ought to make me famous, if I ever get a chance to write a book about it."

Georgie K. stared at him inquiringly.

"I don't know that you will understand, old man," said Gordon, "but here it is. It is simple in one way. Nobody will deny that we come of the earth; well, we are sick and die of the earth. We grow old and weary and drop into our graves, because of the tremendous, though unconscious and involuntary, wear upon nerves and muscles and emotion which is required to keep us here at all. Gravitation kills us all in the end, just as surely as if we fell off a precipice. Gravitation is the destroyer, and gravitation is earth-force. The same monster which produces us devours us. That's so. I hope I shall get a chance to write that book. Clubs are trumps; pass."

"Sure you are well, Doc?" inquired Georgie K., again scowling anxiously.

"Never felt better, didn't I just say so? You are a regular old hen, Georgie K. You cluck at a fellow like a setting hen at one chicken."

Still Doctor Gordon's gloomy face, although he tried to be jocular, did not relax. Going home late that night, or rather early next morning, he laid his hand heavily on James's shoulder.

"Boy, I am about at the finish!" he groaned out.

"Now, see here, Doctor Gordon, can't I be of some assistance if you were to tell me?" asked James. He passed his hand under the older man's arm, and helped him through a snowdrift as if he had been his father. A great compassion filled his heart.

But Gordon only groaned out a great sigh. "No," he said. "Secrecy is the one shield I have. I don't say weapon, but shield. In these latter days we try to content ourselves with shields; and secrecy is the strongest shield on earth. If I were going to commit a crime, I should never even intimate the slightest motive for it to any man living. I should trust no man living to help me through with it."

James felt a vague horror steal over him. He tried to speak lightly to cover it. "I trust there is no question of crime?" he said, laughing.

"Not the slightest," replied Gordon. "I have no intention to use a weapon, but my shield I must stick to. Thank the Lord, you were awake last night, and tonight Clemency is in another room. By the way, I have bought a dog."

"A dog?"

"Yes, a bull terrier, well trained, but he has a voice like a whole pack of hounds. Clemency likes dogs. I will venture that no one comes near the house after this without waking him up."

"You will keep him tied though."

"Yes, unless I get driven too far," replied Gordon grimly.

"Does Mrs. Ewing like dogs?"

"She is as fond of them as Clemency."

When, the next day, the dog arrived James was assured of the fact that both Clemency and Mrs. Ewing did like dogs. They seemed more pleased than he had ever seen them, and the dog responded readily to their advances. He was a splendid specimen of his breed, very large, without a spot on his white coat, and with beautiful eyes. Doctor Gordon had a staple fixed in the vestibule, and the dog was leashed to it at night. "I can't have my patients driven away," he said with a laugh.

That evening Doctor Gordon had a call, and he took Aaron with him. That left James alone with Clemency, as Mrs. Ewing retired almost immediately after Doctor Gordon left.

After the jingle of the sleigh-bells had died away Clemency laid down her work and looked at James. The new dog was lying at her feet. "Uncle Tom bought this dog on account of him," she said. As she spoke, she gave an odd significant gesture over her shoulder as if the man were there, and a look of horror came over her face. Immediately the dog growled, and sprang up, raced to the door, and let forth a volley of howls and barks. "He knows," said Clemency. "Isn't it queer? That dog knows there is something wrong just by the way I spoke and looked."

James himself was not quite so sure. He glanced at the closed shutters. Then he went himself to the door to be sure that it was bolted as usual, and through into the study. Everything was fast, but the dog continued to race wildly back and forth from door to windows, barking wildly, with a slender crest of hair erect on his glossy white back. Emma, the maid, came in from the kitchen, and met James and Clemency in the hall. She looked white, and was trembling. "I know there was somebody about the house," she said.

James hesitated. He thought of a possible patient. Still there had been no ring at the office door. He considered a moment. Then he sent Clemency, the maid, and the dog back into the parlor, and before he opened the outer door of the office he locked the other which communicated with the rest of the house, and put the key in his pocket. Then he threw open the outer door and called, "Anybody there?"

Utter silence answered him. He looked into a black wall of night. It was not snowing, but the clouds were low and thick, and no stars were visible. He called again in a shout, "Hullo there! Who is it?" and obtained no response. Then he closed the door, fastened it, and returned to the living-room. "I guess you were right," he said to Clemency.

"Yes, I think so," said Clemency. She spoke to Emma. "Jack acted so because of something I said to Doctor Elliot," she added. "He thought something was wrong. He is very intelligent." The dog was again lying at her feet.

But Emma shook her head obstinately. She was the middle-aged daughter of a New Jersey farmer, and had lived with the family ever since they had resided in Alton. She had a harsh face, although rather good-looking, "I have been used to dogs all my life," said she, "and I never knowed a dog to act like that unless there was somebody about the house."

"Well, I have done all I could," said James. "I called out the office door, and nobody answered. It could not have been a patient."

"There was somebody about the house," repeated Emma. "Well, I must go and mix up the bread."

When she was gone, Clemency looked palely at James. "Oh," she said, "do you think it could have been that man?"

"No," replied James firmly; "it must have been your gesture. That is a very intelligent dog, and dogs have imagination. He imagined something wrong."

"I hope it was that," said Clemency faintly. "It seems to me I should die if I thought that terrible man were hanging about the house. It is bad enough never to be able to go out of doors."

"Doctor Gordon says I may take you out driving some evening," said James consolingly.

Clemency looked at him with a brightening face. "Did he?"

"Yes."

Then to James's utter surprise Clemency broke down, and began to cry. "Oh," she wailed, "I don't know as I want to go. I am afraid all the time. If we were out driving, and he came up to the horse's head, what could we do?"

"He would get a cut across the face that he would remember," James returned fiercely.

"But he would see me."

"It would be dark."

"He might have a lantern."

"You can wear a thick veil."

Clemency sobbed harder than ever. "Oh, no," she wailed, "I don't want to go so, in the dark, with a thick veil over my face, thinking every minute he may come. Oh, no, I don't want to go."

"You poor little soul," said James, and there was something in his voice which he himself had never heard before. Clemency glanced up at him quickly, and he saw as plainly as if he had been looking in a glass himself in her blue eyes. Instantly emotions of which he had dreamed, but never experienced, leaped up in his heart like flame. He knew that he loved Clemency. What he had felt for her mother had been passionless worship, giving all, and asking nothing. This was love which asked as well as gave. "Clemency," he began, and his voice was hoarse with emotion. She turned her head away, the tears were still on her cheeks, but they were very red, and her cheeks were dimpling involuntarily.

"Well?" she whispered.

"Do you care anything about—me?"

Clemency nodded, still keeping her face averted.

"That means—"

Clemency said nothing.

"That means you love me," James whispered.

Clemency nodded again. Then she turned her head slowly, and gave him a narrow blue glance, and smiled like a shy child.

"I was afraid—" she began.

"Afraid of what, dear?" James put his arm about the girl, and the ashe-blonde head dropped on his shoulder.

"Afraid you—didn't."

"Afraid I didn't care?"

Clemency nodded against his breast.

"I think I must have cared all the time, only at first, when I saw your mother—"

Clemency raised her head immediately and gave it an indignant toss. "There," said she. "I knew it. Very well, if you would rather be my stepfather, you can, only I think you would be a pretty one, no older, to speak of, than I am, and I know my mother wouldn't have you anyway. The idea of your thinking that my mother would get married again anyway, and especially to you," Clemency said witheringly. She sat up straight and looked at James. "I wish your father were a widower, then I would marry him the minute he asked me," said she, "and see how you would like it. I guess you would have a step-mother who would make you walk chalk." Clemency tossed her head again. Then she gave a queer little whimsical glance at James, and both of them burst out laughing, and she was in his arms again, and he was kissing her. "There, that is enough," said she presently. "I once wore out a doll I had kissing her. She was wax, and it was warm weather, and I actually did wear that doll out. The color all came off her cheeks, and she got soft."

"You are not a doll, darling," said James fervently, and he would have kissed her again, but she pushed him away. "No," said she, "I know the color won't come off my cheeks, but I might get soft like that doll. One can never tell. You must stop now. I want to talk to you. It is all right about my mother."

"It was only because I never saw such a woman in all my life before," said James. "I never thought of marrying."

"You would have had to take it out in thinking," said Clemency, "but it is all right. I think myself that my mother is the most wonderful woman that ever lived. I think the old Greek goddesses must have looked just like her. I don't wonder you felt so about her. I don't know as I should have thought much of you if you hadn't. Why, everybody falls down and worships her. Of course I know that I am nothing compared to her. I should be angry if you really thought so."

"I don't think so in one way," James said honestly. "I don't think you are as beautiful as your mother, but I love you, Clemency."

"Well, that will do for me," said Clemency. "No, you need not kiss me again. I think myself I shall make you a better wife than a stepdaughter. You need not think for one minute that I would have minded you as I do Uncle Tom."

"But you will have to when we are married," said James.

Clemency blushed and quivered. "Well, maybe I will," she whispered. "I suppose I shall be just enough of a fool to stay in the house, if you order me, the way I do when Uncle Tom does."

"You shall stay in the house for no man alive when I have you in charge," said James. "Clemency—"

"What?"

"I will take you out now, if you say so. I can protect you."

"I know you can," Clemency said, "but I guess we had better not. You see Uncle Tom doesn't know yet, and he will be coming home, and—"

"I am going to tell him just as soon as he does," declared James.

"I wonder if you had better not wait," Clemency said thoughtfully.

"Wait? Why?"

"Nothing, only poor Uncle Tom is frightfully worried about something now. He worries about that dreadful man, and I am afraid he worries about mother. I don't know exactly what he worries about; but I don't want him worried about anything else."

"I can't see for the life of me why he should worry about this," said James with a piqued air. He was, in fact, considering quite naïvely that he was not a bad match, taking into consideration his prospects, and Clemency evidently needed all the protection she could get.

Clemency understood directly what his tone implied. "Oh, goodness," said she, "of course, as far as you are concerned, Uncle Tom will be pleased. Why shouldn't he? and so will mother. Here you are young and handsome, and well educated, and good, what more could anybody want for a girl, unless they were on the lookout for a ducal coronet or something of that sort? It isn't that, only there is something queer, there must be something queer, about that man, and I don't know how much this might complicate it. I don't know but Uncle Tom might have more occasion to worry."

"I don't see why," said James mystified, "but I'll wait a few days if you say so, only I hate to have anything underhanded, you know.

How about your mother?"

"Please wait and tell her when you tell Uncle Tom," pleaded Clemency. All the time she was completely deceiving the young man. What she was really afraid of was that James himself might run into danger from this mysterious persecutor of hers if the fact of her betrothal became known. "I shall not mind staying in the house at all now," she added. An expression came over her face which James did not understand, which no man would have understood. Clemency was wonderfully skilled at needle-work, and she had plenty of material in the house. She was reflecting innocently how she could begin at once upon some dainty little frills for her trousseau. A delight, purely feminine, filled her fair little face.

"All the same," said James, "I am going to take you out before long. You must have some fresh air."

"I don't mind," said Clemency, then she broke off suddenly. She ran to the farther end of the room, sat down, and snatched a book from the table and opened it in the middle, "It is Uncle Tom," she remarked.

James laughed, crossed the room swiftly, kissed her, then went into the office to greet Doctor Gordon. Doctor Gordon stood by the office fire taking off his overcoat. He looked gloomier than usual. "Who is in there?" he asked, pointing to the living-room wall.

"Your niece," answered James. He felt himself color, but the other man did not notice it.

"Mrs. Ewing has gone to bed?"

"Yes, went directly after you left."

Doctor Gordon's face grew darker. He had tossed his coat over a chair, and stood staring absently at the table with its prismatic lights.

"I know where he is," he said presently in a whisper.

"You mean?"

"Yes," said Doctor Gordon impatiently. "You know whom I mean. I saw him go in—well, no matter where."

"I suspect that he has been hanging about here," said James.

"What makes you think so?"

"The dog barked and acted queer."

"Dogs always did hate him," said Doctor Gordon, with a queer expression. Then he gave himself a shake. Here he said: "Let's have something hot and a smoke." He called to Emma to bring some hot water and sugar and lemons and glasses. Then he produced a bottle from a cabinet in the office, and himself brewed a sort of punch, the like of which James had never tasted before.

"That's my own recipe," said Doctor Gordon, laughing. "Nobody knows what it is, not even Georgie K. But—" he hesitated a little, then he added laughing, "I have left it in my will for Georgie K. I made my will some little time ago."

James felt it incumbent upon himself to say something about Doctor Gordon being still a young man comparatively, and healthy. To his sanguine young mind a will seemed ominous.

"Well, I have not reached the allotted span," Gordon replied, "but healthier men than I have come to their end sooner than they expected, and I wanted to make sure of some things. I wanted especially to make sure that Clemency—Mrs. Ewing has relatives in the West, and—"

James felt somewhat bewildered. He could not quite see what Gordon meant, but he took another sip of the golden, fragrant compound before him, and again remarked upon its excellence.

"That makes me think," said Gordon, evidently glad himself to turn the conversation. "A sip of this will do poor little Clemency good. You say she is in the parlor."

"Yes."

Gordon opened the door and called Clemency, who came with a little reluctance. The girl was afraid of her uncle's eyes. She sidled into the office like a child who had done something wrong. She took her little glass of punch, and never looked at James or her uncle. James, too, did not look at her. He smoked, and almost turned his back upon her. Doctor Gordon looked from one to the other, and his face changed. Clemency slipped out as soon as she could, saying that she was tired. Then Gordon turned abruptly upon James. "There is something between you two, Clemency and you," he said in a brusque voice.

James colored and hesitated.

"Out with it," said Gordon peremptorily.

"Clemency wished—" began James.

"Wished you to keep it secret, of course. Well, she told me herself, poor little soul, the moment she came into the room."

James sat still. He did not know what to do. Finally he said in a stammering voice that he hoped there would be no objection.

"No objection certainly on my part or Mrs. Ewing, if Clemency has taken a fancy to you," replied Doctor Gordon. "But—" he hesitated a moment. "It is only fair to tell you that you yourself may later on entertain some very reasonable objection," Gordon said grimly.

"It is impossible," James cried eagerly. "I have known her only a few weeks, but I feel as if it were a lifetime. Nothing can change me. And as for money, if you mean anything of that kind, I don't care if she hasn't a cent. I have my profession, and my father is well-to-do. Then, besides, I have a little that an aunt, my mother's sister, left me. I can support Clemency."

"It is not that," Gordon said. "Clemency has—at least I think I can secure it to her—a little fortune of her own, and she will have something besides. I was not thinking of money at all."

"Then there can be nothing," James said positively. His sense of embarrassment had passed. He beamed at the older man.

"There can be something else. There is something else," Gordon said gloomily. "I don't know but I ought to tell you, but, the truth is, you know my theory with regard to secrecy. I don't doubt but you can hold your tongue, yet the whole affair is so dangerous, that I dare not, I cannot, tell you yet. I can only say this, that there does exist some obstacle to your marriage with my niece, and your engagement must be regarded by myself in a tentative light. If the time ever comes when you know all, and wish to withdraw, you can do so in my opinion with perfect honor. In the meantime you had better say nothing to any one outside. You had better not even tell Mrs. Ewing. I hope Clemency herself will not. Perhaps when she has had a few hours in which to collect herself, her face will not be quite so tell-tale."

"Nothing whatever can change me," said James, with almost anger.

Gordon shook his head. "I begin to think I may have done you a wrong having you come here at all," he said. "I suppose I ought to have thought of the possibility, but I have had so much on my mind."

"You have done me the greatest good I ever had done me in my whole life," James said fervently.

Gordon rose and shook the young man's hand. "As far as Clemency and I and Mrs. Ewing are concerned," he said, "nothing could have been better. Well, we will hope for the best, my boy." He clapped James on the shoulder and smiled, and James went to his room feeling dizzy with happiness and mystery, and a trifle so with the doctor's punch.

CHAPTER VII

The next morning James was awakened by loud voices coming from the vicinity of the stable. He had not slept very well, and now at dawn felt drowsy, but the voices would not let him sleep. He rose, dressed, and went out in the stable-yard. There he found Doctor Gordon, Aaron, and a strange man, small, and red-haired, and thin-faced, with shifty eyes, holding by the bridle a fine black horse.

"Don't want to buy a horse with a bridle on," Doctor Gordon was saying as James appeared.

"Do you think I'm the man to bear insults?" inquired the little red-haired man with fierceness.

"Insult nothing. It is business," said Gordon.

"That's so," Aaron said, chewing and eyeing the black horse and the red-haired man thoughtfully.

"Well," said the little red-haired man with an air at once of injured innocence and ferocity, "if you want to know why I object to selling this horse without a bridle, come here, and I'll show you." Gordon and Aaron and James approached. The red-haired man slipped the bridle, and underneath it appeared a small sore. "There, that's the reason, and I'll tell you the truth," said the man defiantly. "Here I am trying to sell this darned critter; paid a cool hundred for him, and everybody says jest as you do, won't buy him with the bridle on. Then I takes off the bridle, and they sees this little bile, and there's an end to it. I suppose it's the same with you. Well, good day, gentlemen. You're losin' a darned good trade, but it ain't my fault. Here's an animal I paid a cool hundred for, and I'm offering him for ninety. I'm ten dollars out, besides my time."

"Let me see that sore again," said Gordon. He slipped the bridle and examined the place carefully. Then he looked hard at the horse, which stood with great docility, although he held his head proudly. He was a fine beast, glossy black in color, and had a magnificent tail.

"Make it eighty-five," said Gordon.

"Couldn't think of it."

"I don't know as I want the horse anyway," said Gordon.

"I'll call it eighty-seven and a half," said the little red-haired man.

Gordon stood still for a moment. Then he pulled out his wallet. "Eighty-six and call it square," he said.

"All right," said the red-haired man. "It's a-givin' of him away, but I'm so darned tired of trampin' the country with him, that I'll call it eighty-six, and it's the biggest bargain you ever got in your life in the way of horse flesh. I wouldn't let him go at that figure, but my wife's sick, and I want to get home."

The red-haired man carefully counted over the roll of bank-notes which Doctor Gordon gave him, although it seemed to James that he used some haste. He also thought that he was evidently anxious to be gone. He refused Gordon's offer of breakfast, saying that he had already had some at the hotel. Then he was gone, walking with uncommon speed for such a small man. Aaron, James, and Doctor Gordon stood contemplating the new purchase. James patted him. "He looks like a fine animal," he remarked. Aaron shifted his quid, and said with emphasis, "Want me to hitch up and bring that little red-haired cuss back?"

"Why, what for?" asked Doctor Gordon. "I guess I have made a good trade, Aaron."

"You mark my words, there's somethin' out," said Aaron dogmatically.

"I guess you're wrong this time," said Doctor Gordon, laughing. "Come, Elliot, it is time for breakfast, and we have to drive to Wardville afterward for that fever case."

James followed Gordon into the dining-room. Clemency said good morning almost rudely, then she hid her face behind the coffee-urn. Gordon glanced at her and smiled tenderly, but the girl did not see it. James never looked her way at all. She turned the coffee with apparent concentration. She did not dare look at either of the two men. She had never felt so disturbedly happy and so shy. She had not slept all night, she was so agitated with happiness, but this morning she showed no traces of sleeplessness. There was an unwonted color on her little fair face, and her blue eyes were like jewels under her drooping lids.

They were nearly through breakfast when the door which led into the kitchen was abruptly thrown open, and Aaron stood there. In his hand he flourished dramatically a great streaming mass of black. "Told you so," he observed with a certain triumph. The others stared at him.

"What on earth is that?" asked Gordon.

"That new horse's tail; it comes off," replied Aaron with brevity. Then he chewed.

"Comes off?"

Aaron nodded, still chewing.

Gordon rose from the table saying something under his breath.

"That ain't all," said Aaron, still with an air of sly triumph.

"What else, for Heaven's sake?" cried Gordon.

"Well, he cribs," replied Aaron laconically. Then he chewed.

"That was why he didn't want to take the bridle off?"

Aaron nodded.

Gordon stood staring for a second, then he burst into a peal of laughter. "Bless me if I ever got so regularly done," said he. "Say, Aaron, that was a smart chap. He has talent, he has."

"Aren't you going to try to find him?" asked James.

"Well, we'll keep a lookout on the way to Wardville," said Gordon; "and, Aaron, you may as well put the chestnut in the old buggy and drive Stanbridge way, and see if you can get sight of him."

"He's had a half-hour's start," said Aaron. "You might track a fox, but you can't him."

"I guess you are about right," said Gordon, "but we'll do all we can. However, I think I'll try to get even with Sam Tucker. It's a good chance. I'll drive the new horse to Wardville. Aaron, you just tie that tail on again, and fasten it up so as to keep it out of the mud."

Aaron grinned. "Goin' to get even for that white horse?"

"I'm going to try it."

Gordon was all interest. James regarded him as he had done so many times before with wonder. That such a man should have such powers of assimilation astounded him. He was actually as amused and interested in being done, as he called it, and in trying in his turn to wipe off some old score, as any countryman. He seemed, to the young man, to have little burrows like some desperate animal, into which he could dive, and be completely away from his enemies, and even from himself, when he chose.

He hurriedly drank the remainder of his coffee, and was in his office getting his medicine-case ready. James lingered, in the hopes of getting a word and a kiss from Clemency. But the child, the moment her uncle went out, fled. It was odd. She wanted to stay and have a minute with James alone more than she had ever wanted anything, but it was for just that very reason that she ran away.

James felt hurt. At that time, the mind of a girl, and its shy workings, were entirely beyond his comprehension. He saw no earthly reason why Clemency should have avoided him. He followed Gordon with rather a downcast face into the office, and begun assisting him with his medicines. Gordon himself was too full of interest in the horse trade to remark anything. At times he chuckled to himself. Now and then he would burst out anew in a great peal of laughter. "Hang it all! I don't like to be done any better than any other man, but that little red-haired scamp was clever and no mistake," he said, "showing me that little sore. I believe he had sandpapered the poor beast on purpose. He took me in as neatly as I ever saw anything done in my life. Well, Elliot, you wait and see me get even with Sam Tucker. I have been waiting my chance. About two years ago he worked me, and not half as cleverly as this either. He made me feel that I was a fool. The red-haired one needed the devil himself to get round him, and see through his little game. Sam Tucker sold me, or rather traded with me a veritable fiend of a horse for an old mare. The mare was old, but she had a lot of go in her, and was sound, and the other, well, Sam had bought him for a song, because nobody would drive him, and he had killed two men. He was a white horse with as wicked an eye as you ever saw, and ears always cocked for mischief, like the arch fiend's horns. Well, Sam, he made some kind of a dye, and he actually dyed that animal a beautiful chestnut, and traded him for my old mare. I even paid a little to boot. Well, next morning I sent Aaron down to the store in a soaking rain, and the horse bolted at a white rock beside the road, and the buggy was knocked into kindling wood. Aaron wasn't hurt. He always comes out right side up. But when he came leading that snorting, dancing beast home, the chestnut dye was pretty well off, and I knew him in a minute. Well, he was shot, and I was my old mare and some money out. I wasn't going to have men's lives on my conscience. But this is another matter. Now I've got my chance to get even, and I'm going to get my old mare back."

Presently the two men were out on the road driving the black horse. He went well enough, and seemed afraid of nothing. "There's not much the matter with this animal except the tail and the cribbing, I guess," said the doctor. "As for the tail, that is simply a question of ornament and taste. The cribbing is more serious, of

course, but I guess Sam Tucker won't be in any danger of his life."
They had not gone far before the doctor drew up before a farm-
house on the left. A man with a serious face, thin and wiry, was
coming around the house with a wheelbarrowful of potatoes.
"Hullo, Sam!" called Doctor Gordon. The man left his barrow and
came alongside. James could see that he had a keen eye upon the
horse. "Fine morning," said the doctor.

Sam Tucker gave a grunt by way of assent. He was niggardly
with speech.

"Have you got any more of those Baldwin apples to sell?" asked
Doctor Gordon, to James's intense surprise.

Sam Tucker looked reflectively at the doctor for a full minute,
then gave utterance to a monosyllable. "Bar'l."

"So you've got a barrel to sell," said Gordon.

Sam nodded.

"Well, I'll send my man over for them. They are mighty fine
apples, and Emma said yesterday that we were about out. I suppose
they are the same price."

Sam nodded.

"Seems as if you might take off a little, it is so late, and you
might have them spoiling on your hands," said Gordon, and James
began to wonder if they had come to drive a sharp bargain on
apples instead of horses.

Sam shook his head emphatically. "Same," he said.

"Well, I suppose I've got to pay it if you ask it," said Gordon.
"I can't buy any such apples elsewhere. You've got it your way.
I'll send the money over by Aaron." Doctor Gordon gathered up
the reins, but Sam Tucker seemed to experience a sudden convul-
sion all over his lank body. "Horse," he said.

Doctor Gordon drove on a yard, but Sam, running alongside,
he stopped. "Yes," he said placidly, "horse. What do you think of
him?"

Sam said nothing. He looked at the horse.

"He's the biggest bargain I ever got," said Gordon. "I am going
to hang on to him. Once in a while there is an honest deal in horses.
I am not bringing up anything, Sam. I believe in letting bygones be
bygones, although you did risk my life and my man's. But this time
I am all right." Gordon gathered up the reins again, and again Sam
Tucker stopped him. James barely saw the man's mouth move. He
could not hear that he said anything, but a peculiar glow of eager

greed lit up his long face, and Gordon seemed to understand him perfectly. "You can take your oath not," he said brusquely. "What do you take me for? You have stuck me once, and now you think you are going to do it again. You can bet your life you are not." Again he gathered up the reins. Sam Tucker's face gleamed like a coal. James saw for the first time in its entirety the trading instinct rampant. Again Gordon seemed to understand what had apparently not been spoken. "No, Sam Tucker," he declared almost brutally, "I will not trade back for that old mare you cheated me out of, not if you were to give me your whole farm to boot. I know that old mare. I wasn't the only one that got stuck. She's got the heaves. I know her. No, sir, you don't do me again. I've got a good horse this time, and I mean to hang on to him."

Again Gordon attempted to drive on, and once more Sam stopped him. James felt at last fairly dizzy, when he heard the farmer almost beg Gordon to trade horses, offer him twenty-five dollars to boot, and the apples. He sat in the buggy watching while the mare was led out of the stable, the black horse was taken out of the traces, and the bridle was left on without a remonstrance on Sam's part, and exchanged for a much newer one, while twenty-five dollars in dirty bank-notes were carefully counted out by Sam, and then Gordon jumped into the buggy and drove off. He was quivering with suppressed mirth. "The biter is bitten this time," he said as soon as he was out of hearing of Sam Tucker. Then he made an exclamation of dismay.

"What's the matter?" asked James.

"Well, I have left my whip. I must risk it and go back. I paid a lot for that whip."

Gordon turned and drove back at a sharp trot. When they came alongside the farm fence James saw the whip lying on the ground, and jumped out to get it. He was back in the buggy, and they were just proceeding on their way, when there was a shout, and Sam Tucker came rushing around the house, and held the horse's tail as Aaron had done in the morning. "Comes off," he gasped.

"Of course," said the doctor coolly. "I didn't say it didn't. It's for convenience in muddy weather."

"Cribs," gasped Sam Tucker.

"Yes, a little," said Gordon. "Keep him away from hitching-posts. You didn't say you wanted a horse to hitch. He never cribs when he's driven. Good-day, Sam."

Gordon and James were off again. Gordon was doubled up with merriment, in which James joined. "I'm glad to get behind old Fanny once more," said Gordon. "She's worth two of that other animal! Clemency will be glad to see her again. She felt badly when I traded her. In fact, I wouldn't have done it if I had known how much the child cared for the mare. She used to drive her a lot and pet her. I think it will be perfectly safe for you to take Clemency out driving when there isn't a moon. Fanny is pretty fast when she is touched with the whip, and, though she's gentle, she hasn't much use for strangers. I don't think she would stand a stranger at her head. I think you may go out tonight, if you like. Poor Clemency needs the air. We'll use the team this afternoon, and Fanny will be fresh by evening."

James colored. He remembered how Clemency had avoided him that morning. "Perchance she won't care to go," he said.

"Of course, she will," said Gordon. "She will go, and I want her to, but you must always bear in mind what I told you last night, and—" he hesitated. "Don't do your utmost to make the poor little thing think you are the moon and sun and stars in case you should change your mind," he finished.

"I shall never change my mind," James said hotly.

"You will be justified if you do," Gordon said gravely. "Perhaps you will not. But you are old enough, and ought to have self-command enough to keep your head, and shield the poor child against possible contingencies. You have not known each other very long. It is not possible that she would die of it now, nor you. If you can only keep your head, and meander along the path of love instead of plunging into bottomless depths, it will be better for both of you. I know what I am talking about. I am old enough to be your father. Go slow, for God's sake, if you care about the girl."

"She is the whole world to me," said James.

"Then, go slow! It will be better for her if you are not the whole world to her, until you know what a day may bring forth."

"I don't care what a day brings forth."

"You are tempting the gods," said Gordon. "Elliot, you don't know what you are talking about. I am not treating you fairly not to tell you the whole story, but I don't see my way clear. You must bear in mind what I say. I did not think of any such complication when you came here. I was a fool not to. I know what young people are, and Clemency is a darling, and you have your good points. The amount of it is, if I don't get stuck by Sam Tucker in a horse trade, Fate sticks me in something bigger. I don't see the inevitable, I suppose, because I am so close to it that it is like facing the wall of a precipice all the time. We have to stop here. The woman's daughter is coming down with a fever, which will not kill her, and she will have it to brag of all her life. She will date all earthly events from this fever. Whoa, Fanny!"

That evening James and Clemency went for a drive. It was a clear night, but dark, save for the stars. Clemency had a thick veil over her face, which seemed entirely unnecessary. Directly as they started, she made a little involuntary nestling motion toward the young man at her side. It was as innocent as the nestling of a baby. James put his arm around her. He thought with indignation of Doctor Gordon's warning, as if anything in the world could cause him to change his mind about this dear child who loved him. "You darling!" he whispered. "So you have not thought better of it."

"What do you mean?" Clemency whispered back.

"Why, dear, you have fairly run away from me all day long."

"I was afraid," Clemency whispered, then she put her head against his shoulder, and laughed a delicious little laugh. "I never was in love before, and I don't know how to act," said she.

"Put up your veil," said James.

"Why?"

"I want a kiss."

Clemency put up her veil obediently and kissed him like a child. Then there was a sudden flash of light from a lantern, and a dark form was at the mare's head. But she was true to her master's opinion of her. She gave a savage duck at the man and started violently, so that James was forced to release Clemency and devote his entire attention to driving. Clemency shrank close to him, shivering like one in a chill. "He saw me," she gasped. "It was that same man, and this time he saw me."

CHAPTER VIII

James and Clemency had hardly started upon their drive before there was a ring at the office door, and Doctor Gordon, who was alone there, answered it. He was confronted by a man who lived halfway between Alton and the next village on the north. He had walked some three miles to get some medicine for his wife, who was suffering from rheumatism. He was pathetically insistent upon the fact that his wife did not require a call from the doctor, only some medicine. "Now, see here, Joe," said Gordon, "if I really thought your wife needed a call, I would go, and it should not cost you a cent more than the medicine, but I am dog tired, and not feeling any too well myself, and if her symptoms are just as you say, I think I can send her something which will fix her up all right."

"She is just the way she was last year," said the man. He did not look unlike Gordon, although he was poorly clad, and was a genuine son of the New Jersey soil. His poor clothes, even his skin, had a clayey hue, as if he had been really cast from the mother earth. It was frozen outside, but a reddish crust from the last thaw was on his hulking boots. He spoke with a drawl, which was nasal, and yet had something sweet in it. "I would have came this afternoon, but I was afraid you might have went out," he remarked.

"Yes, I was out," replied Gordon, who was filling out a prescription. The man stooped and patted the bull terrier, which had not evinced the slightest emotion at his entrance.

"Mighty fine dog," said the man.

"Yes, he is a pretty good sort," replied Gordon.

"Shouldn't like to meet him if I had came up to your house an' no one round, and he had took a dislike to me."

"I should not myself," said Gordon. "But he does not dislike you."

"Dogs know me pooty well," said the man. "They ain't no particler likin' for me. Don't want to run and jump an' wag, but they know I mean well, and they mostly let me alone."

"Yes, I guess that's so," said Gordon. "Jack would have barked if he had not known you were all right, Joe."

"Queer how much they know," said the man reflectively, and a dazed look overspread his dingy face with its cloud of beard. If once he became launched upon a current of reflection, he lost his mental bearings instantly and drifted.

"Well, they do know," said Gordon. "Now listen, Joe! You see this bottle. You give your wife a spoonful of the medicine in a glass of water every three hours. Mind, you make it a whole tumbler full of water."

"Yes, sir," replied the man.

"Of course, you need not wake her up if she gets to sleep," said the doctor, "but every three hours when she is awake."

"Yes, sir." The man began fumbling in his pocket, but Gordon stopped him. "No," he said, "put up your pocketbook, Joe. I don't want any money. I get this medicine at wholesale, and it don't cost much."

"I come prepared to pay," said the man. He straightened his shoulders and flushed.

"Oh, well," said Doctor Gordon, "wait. If you need more medicine, or it seems necessary that I should drive over to see your wife, you can do a little work on my garden in the spring, or you can let me have a bushel of your new potatoes when they are grown next summer, or some apples, and we'll call it square. Wait; I don't want any money for that bottle of medicine tonight anyhow. Did you walk over, Joe?"

Joe said that he had walked over. "Aaron might just as well drive you home as not," said Gordon. "The sooner your wife has that medicine the better. How is the baby getting along?"

"First-rate. I'd just as soon walk, doctor."

For answer Gordon opened the door and called Aaron, and told him to hitch up and take the man home.

"Doctor Elliot has gone with the bay," said Aaron. "The teams are about played out, and there's nothin' except the gray."

"Take her then."

"She looked when I fed her jest now as if she was half a mind to balk at takin' her feed," Aaron remarked doubtfully.

"Nonsense! Give her a loose rein, and she'll be all right."

Aaron went out grumbling.

Gordon offered the man a cigar, which he accepted as if it had been a diamond. "I'll save it up for next Sunday, when I've got a little time to sense it," he said. "I know what your cigars be."

Gordon forced another upon him, and the man looked as pleased as a child.

Presently a shout was heard, and Gordon opened the office door.

"Here's Aaron with the buggy," he said.

He stood in the doorway watching, but the gray, instead of balking, went out of the yard with an angry plunge. Gordon shook his head.

"Confound him, he's pulling too hard on the lines," he muttered. Then he closed and locked the office door, and went into the living-room to find it deserted. Gordon called up the stairs. "Have you gone to bed, Clara?" His voice was at once tenderly solicitous and angry.

Mrs. Ewing answered him from above, and in her tone was something propitiating. "Yes, Tom, dear," she called.

Gordon hesitated a moment. His face took on its expression of utmost misery. "Is—the pain very bad?" he called then, and called as if he were in actual fear.

"No, dear," the woman's patient, beseeching voice answered, "not very bad."

"Not very?"

"No, only I felt a little twinge, and thought I had better go to bed. I am quite comfortable now. I think I shall go to sleep. I am sorry to leave you alone all the evening, Tom."

"That's right," called Gordon. His voice rang harsh, in spite of his effort to control it. He threw his arm over his eyes, and fairly groped his way back to his office, stifling his sobs. When he was in his office he flung himself into a chair, and bent his head over his hands on the table, and his whole frame shook. "Oh, my God!" he muttered. "Oh, my God!" He did not weep, but he gasped like a child whom his mother has commanded not to weep. Terrible emotion fairly convulsed him. He struggled with it as with a visible foe. At last he sat up and filled his pipe. The dog had crept close to him, and was nestling against him and whimpering. Gordon patted his head. The dog licked his hand.

The simple, ignorant sympathy of this poor speechless thing nearly unnerved the man again, but he continued to smoke. He looked at the dog, whose honest brown eyes were fixed upon him with an almost uncanny understanding, and reflected how the woman upstairs, who was passing out of his life, had become in a few days so associated with the animal, that after she was gone he could never see him without a pang. He looked about the office, with whose belongings she was less associated than with anything in the house, and it seemed to him that everything even there would have for him, after she had passed, a terrible sting of reminiscence. It seemed to him, as he looked about, as if she were already gone. He was, in fact, suffering as keenly in anticipation as he would in reality. The horror, the worst horror of life, of being left alive with the dead and the associations of the dead was already upon him. Some people are comforted by such associations, others they rend. Gordon was one whom they would rend, whom they did rend. He made up his mind, as he sat there, that he would have to go away from Alton, and enter new scenes for the healing of his spirit, and yet he knew that he should not go: that at the last his courage would assert itself.

He sat smoking, the dog's head on his knee. There was not a sound to be heard in the house. Emma, the maid, had gone away to visit a sick sister. She might not be back that night. So there was absolute silence, even in the kitchen. Suddenly the dog lifted his head and listened to something which Gordon could not himself hear. He watched the dog curiously. The dog gave a low growl of fear and rage, and made for the office door. He began scratching at the threshold, and emitted a perfect volley of barks. It did not sound like one dog, but a whole pack. Gordon, with an impulse which he could not understand, quickly put out the prism-fringed lamp which hung over his table. Then he sprang to the dog, and had the dog by the collar. "Be still, Jack," he said in a low voice, and the dog obeyed instantly, although he was quivering under his hand. Gordon could feel the muscles run like angry serpents under the smooth white hair, he felt the crest of rage along his back. But the animal was so well trained that he barked no more. He only growled very softly, as if to himself, and quivered.

Gordon ordered him to charge in a whisper, and the dog stretched himself at his feet, although it was like the crouch of a live wire. Then Gordon rose and went softly to a window beside the door. The office had very heavy red curtains. It was impossible, since they were closely drawn, that a ray of light from within should have been visible outside. Gordon had reasoned it out quickly when he extinguished the lamp. Whoever was without would have had no possible means of knowing that anything except the dog was in the office, but the light once out, Gordon could peep around the curtain and ascertain, without being himself seen, what or who was about. He had a premonition of what he should see, and he saw it. The stable door was almost directly opposite that of the office. Between the two doors there was a driveway. On this driveway the only pale thing to be seen in the darkness was the tall, black figure of a man standing perfectly still, as if watching. His attitude was unmistakable. The long lines of him, upreared from the pale streak of the driveway, were as plainly to be read as a sign-post. They signified watchfulness. His back was toward the office. He stood face toward the curve of the drive toward the road, where any one entering would first be seen. Gordon, peeping around his curtain, knew the dark figure as he would have known his own shadow. In one sense it had been for years his own shadow, and that added to the horror of it. The man behind the curtain watched, the man in the drive watched; and the dog, crouched at the threshold of the door, watched with what sublimated sense God alone knew, which enabled him to know as much as his master, and now and then came the low growl. Gordon began to formulate a theory in his mind. He remembered suddenly the man whom Aaron had driven home. He realized that the watching man might easily have mistaken him for Gordon himself, going away with his man to make a call upon some patient. He suspected, with an intensity which became a certainty, that the man knew that Clemency and Elliot were out and would presently return, and that it was for them he was watching. All the time he thought of the sick woman upstairs, and was glad that her room faced on the other side of the house. He was in agony lest she should be disturbed.

Doctor Gordon was usually a man of resources, but now he did not know what to do. The dark figure on the park-drive made now and then a precautionary motion of his right arm as he watched, which was significant. Gordon knew that he was holding a revolver in readiness. In the event of Aaron returning alone he would probably be puzzled, and Gordon thought that he might slip away. In the event of James and Clemency returning first, Gordon thought that he knew conclusively what he purposed—a bullet for James, and then away with the girl, unless he was hindered.

Gordon let the curtain slip back into place, and with a warning gesture to the dog, who was ready for action, he tiptoed across the room to the table, in a drawer of which he kept his own revolver. He opened the drawer softly, and rummaged with careful hands. No revolver was there. He made sure. He even opened other drawers and rummaged, but the weapon was certainly missing. He stood undecided for a moment. Then he went softly out of the room, bidding in a whisper the dog to follow. He crept upstairs and paused at a closed chamber door. Then he opened it very carefully. Mrs. Ewing at once spoke. "Is that you, dear?" she said.

"Yes, I wanted to tell you not to be frightened, dear, if you should hear a shot or the dog bark."

There was a rustling in the dark room. Mrs. Ewing was evidently sitting up in bed. "Oh, Tom, what is it?" she whispered.

Gordon forced a laugh. "Nothing at all," he replied, "except there's a fox or something out in the yard, and Jack is wild. I may get a shot at him. Do you know where my revolver is?"

"Why, where you always keep it, dear, in the table drawer in the office."

"I don't seem to see it. I guess I will take your little pistol."

"Oh, Tom, I am sorry, but I know that won't go off. Clemency tried it the other day. You remember that time Emma dropped it. I think something or other got bent. You know it was a delicate little thing."

"Oh, well," said Gordon carelessly, "I dare say I can find my revolver."

"I don't see who could have taken it away," said Mrs. Ewing. "I am sorry about my pistol, because you gave it to me too, dear."

"I'll get another for you," said Gordon. "Those little dainty, lady-like, pearl-mounted weapons don't stand much."

"I am feeling very comfortable, dear," Mrs. Ewing said in her anxious, sweet voice. "You will be careful, won't you, with your revolver, with that dog jumping about?"

"Yes, dear. I dare say I shall not use the revolver anyway, but don't be frightened if you should hear a little commotion."

"No, Tom."

"Go to sleep."

"Yes, I think I can. I do feel rather sleepy."

Gordon closed the door carefully and retraced his steps to the office, the dog at his heels. He slipped the curtain again and looked out. The man still stood watching in the driveway. Gordon had never been at such a loss as to his best course of action. He was absolutely courageous, but here he was unarmed, and he could have no reasonable doubt that if he should go out, he would be immediately shot. In such a case, what of the woman upstairs? And, moreover, what of James and Clemency? He thought of any available weapon, but there was nothing except his own stick. That was stout, it was true, but could he be quick enough with it? His mad impulse to rush out unarmed except with that paltry thing could hardly be restrained, but he had to think of other lives beside his own.

He began to think that the only solution of the matter was the return of Aaron alone. The watching man would immediately realize that he had made some mistake, that he, Gordon, was in the house, or had been left at the home of a patient. He could have no possible reason for molesting the man. He would probably slip aside into a shadow, then make his way back to the road. In such a case Gordon determined that he and Aaron would follow him to make sure that no harm came to James and Clemency. So Gordon stood motionless waiting, in absolute silence, except for the frequently recurring mutter of fear and rage of the dog. As time went on he became more and more uneasy. It seemed to him finally that Aaron should have been back long before. He moved stealthily across the room, and consulted his watch by the low light of the hearth fire. Aaron had been gone an hour. He should have returned, for the mare was a good roadster when she did not balk. Gordon shook his head. He began to be almost sure that the mare had balked. He returned to the window. His every nerve was on the alert. The moment that James and Clemency should drive into the yard, he made ready to spring, but the horrible fear lest it should be entirely unavailing haunted him. If only Aaron would come. Then the man would slip into cover of the shadows, and steal out into the road, and Gordon would jump into the buggy, and he and Aaron would follow him. He knew the man well enough to be sure that he would never venture an attack upon James and Clemency with witnesses. If only Aaron would come! Gordon became surer that the mare had balked. He vowed within himself that she should be shot the next day if she had. Every moment he thought he heard the sound of wheels and horse's hoofs. His nervous tension became something terrible. Once he thought of stealing through the house, and out by the front door, and walking to meet James and Clemency so as to warn them. But that would leave the helpless woman upstairs alone. He dared not do that.

He thought then of going to the front of the house, and watching there, and endeavoring to intercept James and Clemency before they turned into the driveway. But he felt that he could not for one second relax his watch upon the watching man, and he had no guarantee whatever that, at the first sound of wheels, the man himself would not make for the front of the house. Then he thought, as always, of not disturbing the sick woman whose room faced the road. It seemed to him that his only course was to remain where he was and wait for the return of Aaron before James and Clemency. He knew now that the horse must have balked. His only hope was that James and Clemency, since it was such a fine night, and time is so short for lovers, might take such a long drive that even the balky mare might relent. Always he heard at intervals the trot of a horse, which only existed in his imagination. He began to wonder if he should know when Aaron, or Clemency and James, actually did drive into the yard, if he should be quick enough. Suddenly he thought of the dog: that he would follow him, and of what might happen. The dog's chain-leash was on the table. He stole across, got it, fastened it to the animal's collar, and made the end secure to a staple which he had had fixed in the wall for that purpose. As yet no intention of injury to the man except in self-defense was in his mind. If actually attacked, he must defend himself, of course, but he wished more than anything to drive the intruder away with no collision. That was what he hoped for. The time went on, and the strain upon the doctor's nerves was nearly driving him mad. Sometimes the mare balked for hours. He began to hope that Aaron would leave her, and return home on foot. That would settle the matter. But he remembered a strange trait of obstinacy in Aaron. He remembered how he had once actually sat all night in the buggy while the mare balked. The man balked as well as the horse. "The damned fool," he muttered to himself in an agony. The dog growled in response. Then it was that first the thought came to Gordon of what might be done to save them all. He stood aghast with the horror of it. He was essentially a man of peace himself, unless driven to the wall. He was a good fighter at bay, but there was in his heart, along with strength, utter good-will and gentleness toward all his kind. He only wished to go his way in peace, and for those whom he loved to go in peace, but that had been denied him. He began considering the nature of the man whose dark figure remained motionless on the driveway. He knew him from the first. It sounded sensational, his recapitulation of his knowledge, but it was entirely true. It was that awful truth, which is past human belief, which no man dares put into fiction. That man out there had been from his birth a distinct power for evil upon the face of the earth. He had menaced all creation, so far as one personality may menace it. He was a force of ill, a moral and spiritual monster, and the more dangerous, because of a subtlety and resource which had kept him immune from the law. He outstripped the law, whose blood-hounds had no scent keen enough for him. He had broken the law, but always in such a way that there was not, and never could be, any proof. There had not been even suspicion. There had been knowledge on Gordon's part, and Mrs. Ewing's, but knowledge without proof is more helpless than suspicion with it. The man was unassailable, free to go his way, working evil.

Again Gordon thought he heard the nearing trot of a horse, and again the dog growled. Gordon was not quite sure that time that a horse had not passed the house. He told himself in despair that he could not be sure of knowing when James and Clemency came, and again the awful thought seized him, and again he reflected upon the man outside. Suppose, instead of wearing the semblance of humanity, he had worn the semblance of a beast, then his course would have been clear enough. Suppose it were a hungry wolf watching out there, instead of a man, and this man was worse than any wolf. He was like the weir-wolf of the old Scandinavian legend. He had all the cowardly cruelty of a wolf, he was a means of evil, but he had the trained brain of a man.

Gordon thought he heard footsteps, and the man made a very slight motion. Gordon thought joyfully that Aaron had left the balky mare, and had returned, but it was not so. He had heard nothing except the pulsations of the blood in his own overwrought brain.

He wondered if he were really going mad, although all the time his mind was steadily at work upon the awful problem which had been forced upon it. Should any power for evil be allowed to exist upon the earth if mortal man had strength to stamp it out? Suppose that was a poisonous snake out there, and not a man. What was out there was worse than any snake. Gordon reasoned as the first man in Eden may have reasoned; and he did not know whether his reasoning were right or wrong. Meantime, the danger increased every moment. Of one thing he was perfectly sure: he had no personal motive for what he might or might not do. He had reached that pass when he was himself, as far as he himself was concerned, beyond hate of that man outside. It was a principle for which he argued. Should a monster, something abnormal in strength and subtlety and wickedness, something which menaced all the good in the world, be allowed to exist? Gordon argued that it should not. He was driven to it by years of fruitless struggling against this monstrous creation in the shape of man. He had seen such suffering because of him; his whole life had been so turned and twisted this way and that way because of him, that he himself had in the end become abnormal, and mentally askew, with the system of things. He was conscious of it himself. He had been naturally a good, simple, broad-visioned man, full of charity, with almost no subtlety. He had been forced to lead a life which strained and diverted all these good traits. Where he would have been open, he had been secret. Where he would have had no suspicion of any one, his first sight now seemed to be for ulterior motives. He weighed and measured where he naturally would have scattered broadcast. He had been obliged to compress his broad vision into a narrow window of detection. He was not the man he had been. Where he had gazed out of wide doors and windows at life, he now gazed through keyholes, and despised himself for so doing. In order to evade the trouble which had fallen to his lot, he took refuge in another personality. Thomas Gordon was a man whom a happy and untroubled life would have kept from all worldly blemish. Now the gold was tarnished, and he himself always saw the tarnish, as one sees a blur before the eye. Twenty years before, if any one had told him that he would at any period of his life become capable of standing and arguing with himself as to the right or wrong of what was now in his mind, he would have been incredulous. He had in reality become another man. Circumstances had evolved him, during the course of twenty years, into something different, as persistent winds evolve a pliant tree into another than its typical shape. Gordon had lost his type.

As he stood at the window the room grew cold. The hearth fire had died down. He knew that the furnace needed attention, but he dared not quit his post and his argument. He became sure that the maid would not return that night. He knew that Aaron was sitting with his human obstinacy behind the obstinate brute, somewhere on the road. He knew that James and Clemency might at any moment drive in, and he might rush out too late to prevent murder and the kidnapping of the girl. He knew what the man was there for. And he knew the one way to thwart him, but it was so horrible a way that it needed all this argument, all this delay and nearing of danger, before he adopted it.

The increasing cold of the room seemed to act as a sort of physical goad toward action. "By God, it *is* right!" he muttered. Then he looked at the dog crouching still with that wiry intentness before the door. The dog came of a good breed of fighters. He was in himself both weapon and wielder of weapon. He was a concentrated force. His white body was knotted with nerves and muscles. The chances were good if—Gordon pictured it to himself—and again the horror and doubt were over him. He himself had acquired a certain stiffness and lassitude from years, and long drives in one position. He would stand no chance unarmed against a bullet. But the dog—that was another matter. The dog would make a spring like the spring of death itself, and that white leap of attack might easily cause the aim to go wrong. It would be like aiming at lightning. He knew how the dog would gather himself together, all ready for that terrible leap, the second he opened the door. He knew that he might be able to open the door for the leap without attracting the man's attention, faced as he was the other way, if he could keep the dog quiet. He knew how it would be. He could see that tall dark figure rolled on the drive, struggling as one struggles with death, for breath, under the vise-like grip on his throat. Gordon knew that the dog's unerring spring would be for the throat; that was the instinct of his race, a noble race in its way, to seize vice and danger by the throat, and attack the very threshold of life.

Gordon returned to the window. It seemed to him again that he heard a horse's trot. He felt sure that it was not the trot of the gray, who had a slight lameness. He knew the trot of the gray. He became sure that James and Clemency would the next moment enter the drive. He set his mouth hard, crept toward the dog, and patted him. As he patted him he felt the rage-crest rise higher on his back. Gordon bade him be quiet, and slipped his leash from the staple. Then he took it from the collar. He listened again. It seemed to him that his ears could not deceive him. It seemed to him that James and Clemency were coming. He was almost delirious. He fancied he heard their voices and the girl's laugh ring out. Holding the dog firmly by the collar, he rose and very carefully and noiselessly slipped the bolt of the door back. Then he waited a second.

Then as slowly and carefully, still holding the dog by the collar, and whispering commands to hush his growls, he turned the door knob.

Then the thing was done. He flung the door open. He saw the man in the drive, standing with his face toward the road. He had heard nothing. Then he loosened his grasp of the straining dog's collar, and there was a white flash of avenging brute force upon the man. Gordon saw only one leap of the dog before the man was down. A futile pistol shot rang out. Then came the snarl and growl of a fighting dog fastened upon his prey.

CHAPTER IX

When Clemency and James returned from their drive, they saw a glimmer of light between the house and stable. "Aaron is out there with a lantern," whispered Clemency. She sat up straight, leaned into her corner of the buggy, and adjusted her hat and straightened her hair with the pretty young girl motions of secrecy and modesty.

James peered ahead into the darkness through which the lantern moved like a will-o'-the-wisp. "Your uncle is here, too," he said. Then he drew rein with a sudden, "Halloo, what is wrong?" Aaron came forward, leaving the lantern on the ground. It lit weirdly Dr. Gordon, who was kneeling on the ground beside a dark mass, which looked horribly suggestive. Then James saw another dark mass to the right, the balky mare and a buggy.

"Doctor Gordon says you had better hitch to this post here," said Aaron in a sort of hoarse whisper, "and then come to him. He says he needs help, and Miss Clemency, he says, must go around the house and in the front door, and be careful not to let the dog out, but go upstairs, and if her mother is awake, tell her it ain't anything for her to fret about, and Doctor Gordon will be in very soon."

"Oh, Aaron, what is the matter?" said Clemency, in a frightened whisper, as James sprang out of the buggy.

"It ain't nothin'," replied Aaron doggedly. "Jest a man fell coming to the office. Reckon he had a jag on. Doctor says he may have broke a rib. He's doctorin' him. You jest run round the house, and in the front door, Miss Clemency, and don't let out the dog, an' see to your ma."

James assisted Clemency out, and she fled, with a wild glance over her shoulder at the lantern-lit group in front of the office door. While Aaron tied the horse to the post James ran to Doctor Gordon. When he drew nearer the sight became sanguinary in its details, and he could hear from the office the raging growls and howls of the dog. He also heard him leap against the door, as if he would break it down. Gordon had a pail of water and a basin beside him, and he was applying water vigorously to the throat of the prostrate figure. The water in the basin gleamed, in the lantern light, blood red. "Just empty this basin and fill it up from the pail," ordered Gordon in a husky voice, and again he squeezed the reddened cloth over the throat, which James now discerned was badly torn. The man lay doubled up upon himself as limp as a rag.

"No, I don't think so," replied Gordon, as if in answer to an unspoken question, as James, having complied with his request, drew near with the basin of fresh water.

"Was it the dog?" asked James in a low voice.

"Yes, the fool came round to the office door, and—" Gordon stopped with a miserable sigh which was almost a groan, and dipped the cloth in the basin.

"How did you get him off?" asked James.

"I had the whip, and Aaron came in just then with that damned mare. She had balked. I don't think it is the jugular. It can't be. Damn it, how he bleeds! Run into the office, Elliot, and get the absorbent cotton and the brandy. I've got to stop this somehow. Oh, my God!"

James suddenly recognized the man on the ground, and gave an exclamation which Gordon did not seem to notice. "For God's sake, don't let that dog out!" he cried. "Don't risk the office door. Go around the house, the front way! Be quick!"

James obeyed. He rushed around the house, and opened the front door. Immediately Clemency was clinging to him in the dim vestibule. "Mother is asleep. I think Uncle Tom must have given her some medicine to make her sleep. Oh, what is the matter? Who is that man out there, and what ails him, and what ails the dog? I started to go in the office, but he leapt against the door, so I didn't. I was afraid he might get out and run upstairs and wake mother. Oh, what is it all about?"

"Nothing for you to worry about, dear," replied James. "Now you must be a good little girl, and let me go. Your uncle is in a hurry for some things in the office." He put away her clinging arms gently, and hurried on toward the office, but the girl followed him. "If I don't stand ready to shut the door behind you, that dog will be out," she said. All at once a conviction as to something seized her, and she cried out in terror and horror, "Oh, I know it is that man out there, and Jack wants to get at him. I know."

"It is nothing for you to worry about, dear."

"I know. Is he going to die? Is he hurt much?"

"No, your uncle doesn't think so. Don't hinder me, dear."

"No, I won't. I will stand ready and bang the door together after you before Jack can get out. Oh, it is that man!" Clemency was half-hysterical, but she stood her ground. When James opened the office door cautiously and slipped through the opening, she pushed it together with surprising strength. "Don't get bitten yourself," she called out anxiously.

For a moment James thought that he might be bitten, for the dog was so frenzied that he was almost past the point of recognizing his friends. He made a powerful leap upon James, the crest upon his back as rigid as steel, but James snatched at his collar, threw him, and spoke, and the well-trained animal succumbed before his voice. "Charge!" thundered the young man, and the dog obeyed, although still bristling and growling. James hurriedly caught up his leash and fastened him to the staple, then he opened the inner office door, and spoke quickly and reassuringly to Clemency, who was huddled behind it shaking with fear. "He is all right. I have fastened him," he said. "Don't worry. Now I must go and help your uncle."

"He didn't bite you?"

"Oh, no, he knew me the minute I spoke. Sit down here by the fire and don't be frightened; that's a good little girl."

With that James was out by the other door and in the drive beside Gordon, who was still assiduously applying water to the red throat of the prostrate man. "It is beginning to slack up a little," he said hoarsely. "Here, give me the cotton, and see if you can't get a drop of brandy between his teeth. They are clinched, but just now he moved a little. He may be able to swallow. Aaron, put the team into the wagon, and get a mattress and some blankets from the storeroom. Hurry, he may come to himself any minute, and he must not stay here any longer than necessary." Gordon was working fiercely as he spoke, and James took the cork from the brandy flask, and attempted to force a little between the man's clinched teeth. Aaron hurried into the stable and lit another lantern, and went about executing his orders. James, kneeling over the prostrate man, attempting to minister to him, saw the face fully in the glare of the lantern. The unconscious face did not look as evil as he remembered it. He even had a doubt if it were the face of the man who had that evening stood at his horse's head, and so terrified Clemency. Then he became convinced that it was the same. There could be no mistaking the features, which were unusually regular and handsome, but with a strange peculiarity of lines. It seemed to James that, even while the man was unconscious, all his features presented slightly upturned lines as of bitter derision, intersected with downward lines of melancholy. All these lines were very delicate, but they served to give expression. He looked like a man who had suffered and made others suffer for his sufferings, with a cruel enjoyment at the spectacle. It was a strange face, but not an evil one. However, after James had succeeded in forcing a few drops of brandy, which were met with convulsive swallowing, between the man's teeth, he moved again, and his eyes opened, and immediately the evil shone out of the face like a malignant flame in a lamp. Knowledge of, and delight in, evil gleamed out of the sudden brightness of the man's great eyes. Then the evil seemed to leap to rage, as a spark leaps to flame. He tried to raise himself, and cursed in a choking voice. He seemed awake most fully to consciousness, and to know exactly what had happened. The dog in the office sent forth a perfect volley of barks. The man had been obliged to sink back, but his right hand fumbled feebly for his pocket.

"It is not there," Gordon said coolly.

"Shoot him, you—or—" croaked the man in his voice of unnatural rage.

"Time enough for that," said Gordon. He spoke coolly, but James saw him shaking as if with the ague. He was deadly white, and his whole face looked drawn and withered. Aaron came leading the team harnessed to the wagon out of the stable. He had brought down the mattress and blankets, as the doctor had directed, and the three men after the rude bed had been made in the wagon lifted the man thereon. He seemed to be conscious, but his muttering was so weak as to be almost inaudible, save for occasional words.

After he was in the wagon Gordon, turning to James, said: "You had better go in the house and stay with the women. Aaron will go with me. I shall take this man to the hotel, to Georgie K.'s."

A perfect volley of mumbled remonstrances came from the prostrate figure in the wagon. Gordon seemed to understand him. "No, I shall not take you there," he said, "but to the hotel. You will be better cared for. I know the proprietor."

He got in beside the man, and seated himself on the floor of the wagon. Aaron mounted to the driver's seat.

"Tell Clemency and her mother not to worry if they are awake," Gordon called to James as the horses started.

James said yes and went into the house. He entered through the office door, and directly Clemency was in his arms, all trembling and half-weeping. "Oh, what has happened? Has Uncle Tom taken him away?" she quavered.

"Hush, dear, you will wake your mother. Yes, he has taken him away."

"What was the matter, tell me."

"He was unconscious. He had fallen."

"He came to. I heard him speak. Were any bones broken?"

"No, I think not. You must go to bed; it it very late, dear."

Clemency had put fresh wood on the hearth, and the little place was all a-waver and a-flicker with firelight. Grotesque shadows danced over the walls and ceiling, and sprawled uncertainly on the floor. Clemency looked up in James's face, and her own had a shocked whiteness and horror, in spite of the tenderness in his. "Tell—" she began.

"What, dear?"

"Was it—that man?"

James hesitated.

"Tell me," Clemency said imperiously.

"Yes, I think it was."

Clemency glanced as if instinctively at the dog, lying asleep in a white coil on the hearth. "What was the matter with him?" she asked in a hardly audible voice.

"He had fallen, dear, and was unconscious."

"Nothing—" Clemency glanced again at the dog, and did not complete her question.

"He had recovered consciousness," James said hastily.

"Then he is not going to die." It was impossible to say what kind of relief was in the girl's voice, but relief there was.

"I see no reason why he should. I don't think your uncle thought he would die."

"Where have they taken him?"

"To the hotel. Now, Clemency dear, you must put all this out of your mind and go to bed."

Clemency obeyed like a child. She kissed James, took a candle, and went upstairs.

James went into his own room, but he did not undress or go to bed. Instead, he sat at the window facing the street and stared into the darkness, watching for Doctor Gordon's return. He sat there for nearly two hours, then he heard wheels, and saw the dark mass of the team and wagon lumber into sight. He ran through the house, and was in the drive with a lantern when the team entered. "Have you been waiting for us, Elliot?" called Doctor Gordon's tired voice.

"Yes, I thought I would."

"I stayed until I was sure he was comfortable," said Gordon. He clambered over the wheel of the wagon like an old man. When he was in the office with James, and the lamp was lit, he sank into a chair, and looked at the younger man with an expression almost of despair.

"He is not going to die of it?" asked James hesitatingly.

"No," cried Gordon, "he shall not!" He looked up with sudden, fierce resolution and alertness. "Why should he die?" he demanded. "He is far from being old or feeble. His vitals are not touched. Why on earth should you think he would die?"

"I see no reason," James replied hastily, "only—"

"Only what, for God's sake?"

"I thought you looked discouraged."

"Well, I am, and tired of the world, but this man is going to live. See here, boy, suppose you see if there is any hot water in the kitchen, and we'll have something to drink, then we will go to bed, and God grant we don't have a night call."

After Gordon had drank his face lightened somewhat, still he looked years older than he had done at dinner time, with that awful aging of the soul, which sometimes comes in an instant. When finally he went upstairs James noticed how feebly he moved. It was on his tongue's end to offer to assist him, but he did not dare.

The next morning, before James was up, he heard the rapid trot of a horse on the drive, and wondered if Doctor Gordon had had a call so early. When the breakfast-bell rang only Clemency was at the table. The maid had returned in season to get breakfast, and was waiting with a severely interrogative face.

She had noticed blood on the frozen surface of the drive and had stood surveying it before she entered. She had asked Clemency if anything had happened, and the girl had told her that a man had fallen near the office door on the preceding evening and been injured, and Doctor Gordon had taken him home.

"What's the man's name?" Emma had inquired sharply.

"I don't know," said Clemency, and indeed she did not know,

but there was something secretive in her manner. Emma set her mouth hard and tossed her head. Curiosity was almost a lust with her. She was always enraged when it was excited and not gratified.

When James entered, she glanced severely at him and then at Clemency, as she passed the muffins. She suspected something between them, and she was baffled there.

"Has Doctor Gordon gone out?" James asked.

"Yes, he went right out as soon as he got up. Just had a cup of coffee; wouldn't wait for breakfast," replied Emma in a nipping tone.

Neither Clemency nor James made any comment. Both knew where he had gone, and Emma, seeing that they both knew, grew more hostile than ever. Her manner of serving the beefsteak was fairly warlike.

After breakfast Aaron told James of some parting instructions which Gordon had left with him. He had the team harnessed, and was to take James to visit certain patients.

James went off on a long drive across the country, calling on his way at the scattered houses of the patients. He did not return until noon, just before the luncheon-bell rang. Entering by the office door he found Gordon sitting before the hearth-fire, smoking, and staring gloomily at the leaping flames. He looked up when James entered, said good morning in an abstracted fashion, and asked some questions about the patients whom he had visited. James hesitated about inquiring for the man who had been injured the night before, but finally he did so. The dog had sprung up to greet him, and between his pats on the white head and commands of "Down, sir, down!" he asked as casually as he could if Gordon had seen his patient who had fallen in the drive the night before, and how he was. Gordon turned upon James a face of such fierce misery that the younger man fairly recoiled. "He isn't going to die?" he cried.

"No, he is not going to die. He shall not die!" Gordon replied with passionate emphasis. Then he added, in response to James's wondering, half-frightened look, "I have been there all the morning. I have just come home. I have left everything for him. I don't dare get a nurse. I am afraid. He may talk a good deal. Georgie K. is with him now. I can trust him, but I can't trust a nurse. I am going back after luncheon, and you may go with me. I would like you to see him."

"Does he seem to be very ill?" James asked timidly.

"Not from the—the—wound," replied Gordon, "but I am afraid of something else."

"What?"

"Erysipelas. I am afraid of that setting in. In fact, I am not altogether sure that it has not. He is an erysipelas subject. He has told me of two severe attacks which he has had. When he fell he got an abrasion of the cheek. That looks worse than the—the—wound. I should like you to see him. You have seen erysipelas cases, of course, in your hospital practice."

"Oh, yes."

"There is the bell for luncheon. We will go directly afterward."

James wondered within himself at the feverish haste with which Gordon swallowed his luncheon, frequently looking at his watch. He was actually showing more anxiety over this man who had hounded him, of whom he had lived in dread, than James had seen him show over any patient since he had been with him. It seemed to him inconsistent. Mrs. Ewing did not come down to luncheon; Clemency said that she was not feeling as well as usual but Gordon did not seem much disturbed even by that. He gave Clemency some powders, with instructions how to administer them to the sick woman before he left, but he did not show concern, and did not go upstairs to see her. Clemency herself looked pale and anxious.

She found a chance to whisper to James before he went. "Is that man very much hurt?" she said close to his ear.

"Hush, dear. I am afraid so."

"Uncle Tom seems terribly worried. I have never seen him so worried even over mother, and he doesn't seem worried about her now. Oh, James, she is suffering frightfully, I know." Clemency gave a little sob. Then Gordon's voice was heard calling imperiously, "Elliot, come along!" James kissed the poor little face tenderly, and whispered that she must not worry, that probably the powders would relieve her mother, and then that she herself had better lie down and try to get a little sleep, and hurried out.

Gordon was seated in the buggy, waiting for him. "I don't want to lose any time," he said brusquely as James got in beside him. "Even a few minutes sometimes work awful changes in a case like this. If he is no worse I will leave you with him, and make a call on Mrs. Wells. I haven't seen her today, and yesterday it looked like pneumonia, then there is that child with diphtheria at the Atwaters'. I ought to go there myself, but if he is worse you will have to go, and to a few others, and I must stay with him."

Gordon drove furiously. Heads appeared at windows; people on the street turned faces of wonder and alarm after him. It was soon noised about Alton that there had been a terrible accident, that somebody was at the point of death, but of that Gordon and James knew nothing.

When they arrived at the hotel, Gordon, after he had tied his horse, took his medicine-case, and, followed by James, entered, and went directly upstairs to a large room at the back of the hotel. This room was somewhat isolated in position, having a corridor on one side and linen closets on another, it being a corner apartment with two outer walls. Gordon opened the door softly and entered with James behind him. The bed stood between the two west windows. It was a northwest room. The afternoon sun had not yet reached it. It was furnished after the usual fashion of country hotel bedrooms. It was clean and sparse, and the furniture had the air of having a past, of having witnessed almost everything which occurs to humanity. It seemed battered and stained, though not with wear, but with humanity. The old-fashioned black walnut bedstead in which the sick man lay seemed to have a thousand voices of experiences. A great piece was broken off one corner of the footboard. The wound in the wood looked sinister. Directly opposite the bed stood the black walnut bureau, with its swung glass. The glass was cracked diagonally, and reflected the bed and its occupant with an air of experience. Gordon went directly to his patient. Beside him sat Georgie K. He looked at the two doctors and shook his head gravely. His great blond face was unshaven and paled with watching. Nobody spoke a word. All three looked at the man in the bed, who lay either asleep, or feigning sleep, or in a stupor. Gordon felt for his pulse softly, with keen eyes upon his face. This face was unspeakably ghastly. The throat was swathed in bandages. There was one tiny spot of red on the white of the linen. The man's eyes were rolled upward. Around an abrasion on the cheek, which glistened oily with some unguent which had been applied to it, was a circle of painful red clearly defined from the pallor of the rest of the cheek.

Gordon spoke. "How do you feel?" he asked of the man, who evidently heard and understood, but did not reply. He simply made a little motion of facial muscles, of shoulders, of his whole body under the bed-clothes, which indicated rage and impatience.

"Does that place on your cheek burn?" asked Gordon.

Again there was no answer, this time not even any motion.

"Have you any pain?" asked Gordon. The man lay motionless. "Is there any one in the parlor?" Gordon asked abruptly of Georgie K.

"No, Doc. You can go right in there."

Gordon beckoned to James, and the two went downstairs, and entered the room of the wax flowers and the stuffed canary.

"It looks like erysipelas," Gordon said with no preface.

James nodded.

"All I have done so far, in the absence of any positive proof of the truth of that diagnosis, is to apply what you will think an old woman's remedy, but I have known it to give good results in light cases, and I did not like to resort to the more strenuous methods until I was sure of my ground, for fear of complications. I applied a little mutton tallow, and that was all, but the inflammation has increased since I saw him. It now looks to me like a clearly defined case of erysipelas."

"It does to me," said James.

"So far—the—wound in the throat seems to be doing well," said Gordon gloomily. Then he looked at the younger physician with an odd, helpless expression. "His life must be saved," said he. "Which do you prefer of the two methods of treating the disease—that is, of the two primary ones? Of course, there are methods innumerable. I may have grown rusty in my country practice. Do you prefer the leaches, the nitrate of silver, the low diet, or the reverse?"

"I think I prefer the reverse."

"Well, you may be right," said Gordon, "and yet you have to consider that this is a man in full vigor," he added, "that presumably he has considerable reserve strength upon which to draw. Still if you prefer the other treatment—"

"I have seen very good results from it," said James. He was becoming more and more astonished at the older man's helpless, almost appealing, manner toward himself. "What is the man's name?" he asked.

"I don't know what name he has given here," Gordon replied evasively. "I will tell you later on what his name is."

Suddenly the parlor door was flung open, and a woman appeared. She was middle-aged, very large, clad in black raiment, which had an effect of sliding and slipping from her when she moved. She kept clutching at the buttons of her coat, which did not quite meet over her full front. She brought together the ends of a black fur boa, she reached constantly for the back of her skirts, and gave them a firm tug which relaxed the next moment. Her decent black bonnet was askew, her large face was flushed. She had been a strapping, handsome country girl once; now she was almost indecent in her involuntary exuberance of coarse femininity.

"How do you do, Mrs. Slocum?" Doctor Gordon said politely.

James rose, Gordon introduced him. Mrs. Slocum did not bow, she jerked her great chin upward, then she spoke with really alarming ferocity. "Where has my boarder went? That's what I want to know. That's what I have come here for, not for no bowin's and scrapin's. Where has my boarder went?"

A keen look came into Gordon's face. "I don't know who your boarder is, Mrs. Slocum," he said.

CHAPTER X

Mrs. Slocum looked at the doctor with a wide gape of surprise. "Thought you knew," said she. "His name is Meserve, Mr. Edward Meserve, and if he has come and went, and not told where, he was good pay, and if he was took sick whilst he was to my house, I could have asked twice as much as I did before. I'd like to know what right you had to take my boarder to the hotel. He was my boarder. He wan't your boarder. I want him fetched right back. That's what I have came for."

"Mrs. Slocum," said Gordon in a hard voice, "Mr. Meserve is too sick to be moved, and his disease may be contagious. You might lose all your other boarders, and whether he recovers or not, you would be obliged to fumigate your house, and have his room repapered and plastered."

"He's got money enough to pay for it," Mrs. Slocum said doggedly.

"How do you know?"

"You think he ain't?"

Gordon looked imperturbable.

"He always paid me regular, and he ain't been to meals or to home nights two-thirds of the time."

Gordon said nothing.

"You mean if my other boarders went, and the room had to be done over, he ain't got money enough to make it good?"

Gordon said nothing. The woman fidgeted. "Well," said she, "if there's any doubt of it, mebbe he *is* better off here." Suddenly she gave a suspicious glance at Gordon. "Say," said she, "the room here will have to be done over. Who's goin' to pay for that?"

"The room is isolated," replied Gordon briefly.

The woman stared. She evidently did not know the meaning of the word.

"Well," said she at last, "if the room *is* insulted, it will have to be done over. Who's going to pay for that?"

"I am."

"Well, I don't see why you couldn't pay *me* for that as well as Mr. Evans."

"Don't you?"

"No."

"Well, I do. Now, Mrs. Slocum, I really have no more time to waste. Mr. Meserve is a very sick man, and I have to go to him. I came down here to consult with my assistant, and you have hindered us. Good-day!"

But the woman still stood her ground. "I'm goin' to see him," she said. "He's my boarder."

"You will do so at your own risk, and also, if your call should prove injurious to him, at a risk of being indicted for manslaughter, besides possibly catching the disease."

"You say it's ketchin'?"

"I said it might be. We have not yet entirely formed our diagnosis."

The woman stared yet again. Then she turned about with a switch which disclosed fringy black petticoats and white stockings. "Well, form your noses all you want to," said she. "You have took away my boarder, an' if he gits well, and it ain't ketchin', I'll have the law on ye."

Gordon drew a deep breath when the door closed behind her. "It seems sometimes to me as if comedy were the haircloth shirt of tragedy," he said grimly. "Well, Elliot, we will go upstairs and begin the fight. I am going to fight to the death. I shall remain here tonight. You will have to look after my other patients when you leave here. I am sorry to put so much upon you."

"Oh, that's all right," said James, following Gordon upstairs. But as he spoke he wondered more and more that this man, after what he had known of him, should be of more importance to Gordon than all others.

Even during the short time they had been downstairs the angry red around the abrasion on the cheek had widened, and widened toward the head. Gordon opened his medicine-case and took out a bottle and hairbrush and commenced work. Directly the entire cheek was blackened with the application of iron. Georgie K. had brought glasses, and medicine had been forced into the patient's mouth. "Now go and have some eggnog mixed, Georgie K.," said Gordon, "and bring it here yourself, if you will. I hate to trouble you."

"That's all right, Doc," said Georgie K., and went.

James remained only a short time, since he had the other calls to make. He returned quite late to find that dinner had been kept waiting for him, and Clemency in her pretty red gown was watching. Mrs. Ewing had not come down all day. "Mother says she is easier," Clemency observed, "only she thinks it better to keep perfectly still." Clemency said very little about the man at the hotel. She seemed to dread the very mention of him. She and James spent a long evening together, and she was entirely charming. James began to put behind him all the mystery and dark hints of evil. Clemency, although fond, was as elusive as a butterfly. She had feminine wiles to her finger tips, but she was quite innocent of the fact that they were wiles. It took the whole evening for the young man to secure a kiss or two, and have her upon his knee for the space of about five minutes. She nestled closely to him with a little sigh of happiness for a very little while, then she slipped away, and stood looking at him like an elf. "I am not going to do that much," said she.

"Why not, darling?"

"Because I am not. It is silly. I love you, but I will not be silly. I want only what will last. The love will last, but the silliness won't. We are going to be married, but I shall not want to sit on your knee all the time, and what is more, you will not want me to. Suppose we should live to be very old. Who ever saw a very old woman sitting on her very old husband's knee? The love will last, but that will not. We will not have so very much of that which will not last."

For all that, James caught Clemency and kissed her until her soft face was crimson, but he said to himself, when he was in his own room, that never was a girl so wise, and how much more he wanted to hold her upon his knee—as if he had not already held her there—and yet she was not coquettish. She was simply earnest, with an odd, wise, childlike earnestness.

Early the next morning James went to the hotel, and found Gordon haggard and intense, sitting beside his patient, who was evidently worse. The terrible red fire of Saint Anthony had mounted higher, and settled lower. "It has attacked his throat now," Gordon said in a whisper. "I expect every minute it will reach his brain. When it does, nobody but you and I must be with him, not even Georgie K. He is getting some rest. He was up half the night, bless him! But when it reaches the brain two will be needed here, and the two must be you and I. Take this list, and make the calls as quickly as you can, and come back here." James, with a last glance at the black and swollen face of the man, who now seemed to be in a state of coma, obeyed. He hurried through his list, and returned. He found no apparent change in the patient, and tried to persuade Gordon to take a little rest, but the elder man was obdurate. "No" he said, "here I stay. I have had a bit to eat and drink. You go down yourself and get something, then come back. The crisis may arrive any second. Then I shall need you."

The fire had outstripped the blackness on the man's cheek toward the temple. One eye was closed.

When James returned after a hurried lunch, he heard a loud, terrible voice in the room. Outside the door a maid stood with a horrified face listening. James grasped her roughly by the shoulder. "Get out of this," he ordered. "If I find you or any one else here listening, you'll be sorry for it."

The maid gasped out an excuse and fled. James tried the door, but it was locked. "Is that you, Elliot?" called Gordon above the other awful voice.

"Yes."

The door was unlocked, and James sprang into the room, but he was hardly quick enough, for the man was almost out of bed, when the two doctors forced him back with all their strength. Then he sat up and raved, and such raving! James felt his very blood cold within him. Revelations as of a devil were in those ravings. Once in a while James opened the door cautiously to be sure that no one was listening. The raving man reiterated names as of a multitude. Gordon's was among them, and many names of women, one especially—Catherine. He repeated that name more frequently than the others, but the others were legion. There was something indescribably horrible in hearing this repetition of names of unknown people, accompanied with statements beyond belief regarding them and the raving man. Gordon's face was ghastly, and so was the younger doctor's. "Look and see if any one is listening, for God's sake," Gordon gasped, after one terrific outburst, and James looked, but Georgie K. was keeping watch that nobody approached the door.

James never knew how long he was in that room with Gordon listening to those frenzied ravings, and striving with him to keep the man from injuring himself. The daylight waned, James lighted a lamp. Then a mighty creaking was heard outside, and Georgie K., himself bearing a great supper tray, knocked at the door. "It's me, and I brought you something," he shouted, and then they heard his retreating footsteps. Much delicacy was there in Georgie K., and much affection for Doctor Gordon.

James brought in the tray, and now and then he and Gordon took advantage of a slight lull to take a bite, but neither had any desire for food. It was only the instinctive sense that they must keep up their strength in order that nobody else should hear what they were hearing, that forced them to eat and drink. Well into the evening the ravings stopped suddenly, the man fell back upon his pillow, and lay still. James thought at first that all was over, but presently stertorous breathing began.

"Now get Georgie K. up," Gordon said hoarsely. "There is no further need for us to be alone, and there will be directions to be given."

James went out and found Georgie K. sitting up in his barroom.

"Doctor Gordon wants you," he said.

"How is he?" asked Georgie K., following James.

"Dying."

Georgie K. made an indescribable sound in his throat as the two men ascended the stair.

The man was a long time dying. It seemed to James as if that awful struggle of the soul for release from the body would never cease. He knew, or thought he knew, that there was no suffering to the dying man, but, after all, the sounds as of suffering seemed almost to prove it. Gordon whispered for a while to Georgie K., as if the dying man might be disturbed by audible speech. Then Georgie K. tiptoed out in his creaking boots, and James knew that some arrangements were to be perfected for the last services to the dead. Gordon stood over the bed, with his own face as ghastly as that of its occupant. James dared not speak to him.

It was midnight when the dreadful breathing ceased, and there was silence. Georgie K. had returned. The three living men looked at one another with ghastly understanding of what had happened, then they hastily arranged some matters. The dead man was decently composed and dressed, his throat swathed anew in linen handkerchiefs, and another handkerchief laid over the discolored face, which had in death a strange peace, as if relieved of an uneasy and wearing tenant. Before Georgie K. went out, the village undertaker had been summoned, and had been waiting for some time in the parlor with a young assistant. They mounted the stairs bearing some appurtenances of their trade. Gordon addressed the undertaker briefly, giving some directions, then he motioned to James, and they passed out. Georgie K. remained in the room. He prevented the undertaker from removing the linen swathe on the dead man's throat. "Doc says it's catching," he said, and the undertaker drew back quickly.

When Gordon and James were in the buggy on the way home, Gordon all at once gave a great sigh, like that of a swimmer who yields to the force of the current, or the fighter who sinks before his opponent. "I'm about done, too," he said. "Here, take the lines, Elliot."

James took the reins and looked anxiously at his companion's face, a pale blue in the moonlight. "You are not ill?" he said.

"No, only done up. For God's sake let me rest, and don't talk till we get home!" James drove on. Gordon's head sank upon his breast, and he began to breathe regularly. He did not wake until James roused him when they reached home.

The next morning before breakfast James was awakened by a loud voice in the office, the high-pitched one of a woman. He recalled how exhausted Doctor Gordon had been the night before, and rose and dressed quickly. When he entered the office Gordon was sitting huddled up in his old armchair before the fire, while bolt upright beside him sat Mrs. Slocum, discoursing in loud and angry tones, which Gordon seemed scarcely to heed. When James entered she turned upon him. "Now I'll see if I can git anythin' out of you," she said. "He" (pointing to Gordon) "don't act as if he was half-alive. I'm goin' to have my rights if I have to go to law to git 'em. Doctor Gordon took away my boarder. And if I'd had him sick and die to my house, I could have got extra. Now what I want is jest this, an' I'm goin' to hev it, too! Doctor Gordon said Mr. Meserve didn't have money. I don't know nothin' about that. I ain't went through his pockets, but his trunk is to my house, and there's awful nice men's clothes into it, and I mean to hev 'em. That ain't nothin' more'n fair. That's what I hev came here for, jest as soon as I heard the poor man had passed away. I left my daughter to git the breakfast for the boarders, and I hev came here to see about that trunk, and hisn's clothes."

James laughed. "But, Mrs. Slocum," he said, "what on earth do you want with men's clothes? You can't wear them."

To his intense surprise the great face of the woman suddenly reddened like that of a young girl, but the next moment she gave her head a defiant toss, and stared boldly at him. "What if I can't?" said she. "There's other men as can wear 'em, and they'll jest fit Bill Todd. He's been boardin' with me five year, and if he wants to git married and save his board bill, it's his business and mine and nobody else's."

James turned to Gordon, who seemed prostrated before this feminine onslaught. "Do you object to this woman's having the trunk?" he asked.

Gordon made an effort and roused himself. "She can have it after I have examined it for papers," he said.

"There ain't a scrap of writin' in the trunk," Mrs. Slocum vociferated. "Me an' my boarder hev looked. There ain't no writin' an' no jewelry, an' no money. He used to carry his money with him, and he had a bank book in his pocket, and a long, red book he used to git money out of the bank. I've seen 'em. Doctor Gordon said he didn't have no money. He did hev money. Once he left the long, red book on his bureau, and I looked in it, and the leaves that are as good as money wan't a quarter torn out. I know he had money, an' I've been cheated out of it. But all I ask is that trunk."

"For God's sake take the trunk and clear out," shouted Gordon with unexpected violence, "but if there is a scrap of written paper in that trunk, and you keep it, you'll be sorry."

"There ain't," said the woman with evident truthfulness. She rose and clutched at the back of her skirt, and tugged at her boa and coat. "Thank you, Doctor Gordon," said she. "When is the funeral goin' to be?"

"Tell her tomorrow at two o'clock at the hotel, and tell her to leave," said Gordon, and his voice was suddenly apathetic again.

When the woman had gone Gordon turned to James. "How comedy will prick through tragedy," he said.

"Yes," James answered vaguely. He looked anxiously at Gordon, whose eyes had at once a desperate and an utterly wearied appearance. "I will make all the arrangements for the funeral, if you wish, Doctor Gordon," he said. "I know the undertaker, and I can manage it as well as you. You look used up."

"I am pretty nearly," muttered Gordon. Then he gave an almost affectionate glance at James. "Do you think you can manage it?" he said.

James smiled. "It is a new thing to me, but I have no doubt I can," he replied.

"You cannot imagine what a weight you would take off my shoulders. Don't spare money. See to it that everything is good and as it should be. The bills are to be sent to me."

Gordon answered an unspoken question of James. "Yes," he said, "he had money, a considerable fortune, and he has no heirs—at least, I am as sure as I need be that he has none. In his pockets were two bank books, small check books, and a security register book. I have done them up in a parcel. See to it that they are buried with him."

"But," said James.

"Oh, yes, I know. Sooner or later there will be advertisements in the papers, and that sort of thing, but that will pass. God knows I would not touch his money with the devil's pitchfork, nor allow anybody whom I loved to touch it. Let him be buried under the name by which he was known here. It is not the name, needless to say, on the bank books. While living under other than his rightful name, he must have gone to New York in person to supply himself with cash. There was some two hundred dollars in bank notes in his wallet. That is with the other things. Let the whole be buried with him, and see to it that Drake does not discover it. You had better take the parcel now. Open the right drawer of the table, and you will find it in the corner. Then, after breakfast, you had better see Drake at once. I will attend to the patients today."

"You are not able."

"Able is a word which I have eliminated from my vocabulary as applied to myself."

The funeral, which was held the next afternoon in the parlor of the hotel, was at once a ghastly and a grotesque function. The two doctors, the undertaker and his assistant, Georgie K. and the bartender, and Mrs. Slocum with a female friend, and a man, evidently the boarder to whom she had referred, were the only persons present. The boarder wore a hat which had belonged to the dead man. It was many sizes too large for his grayish blond, foolish little head, and, when he put it on, it nearly obscured his eyes. Mrs. Slocum sniffed audibly through the service, which was short, being conducted by the old Presbyterian clergyman of Alton. He hardly spoke above a whisper of "the stranger who had passed from our midst into the beyond." His concluding prayer was quite inaudible. Mrs. Slocum had brought a bouquet of cheerful pink geraniums from her window plants, which on the top of the closed black casket made an odd spot of color and life in the dim room. Among the blossoms were some rose-geranium leaves, whose fragrance seemed to mantle everything like smoke. While the clergyman conducted the inaudible services loud voices were heard in the barroom, and the yelp of a dog. On one side of the house was the hush of death, on the other the din of life. James wondered what the clergyman found to say: all that he had distinguished was the expression, "The stranger within our midst."

It all seemed horribly farcical to him. The dead man in his casket had no personality for him; the sniffs of Mrs. Slocum, her boarder with the hat, assumed, in his eyes, the character of a "Punch and Judy" show. But along with that feeling came the realization of a most terrible pathos. He felt a sort of pity for the dead man, whose very personality had become nothing to him, and the pity was the greater because of that. It became a pity for the very scheme of things, for man in the abstract, born perhaps, through no fault of his own, to sin and misery, both miserable and causing misery throughout his life, and then to end in the grave, and vanish from the sight and minds of other men. He felt that it would not be so sad if it were sadder, if Mrs. Slocum's sniffs had come from her heart, and not from her sentimentality. He felt that a funeral where love is not is the most mournful function on earth. Then, too, he felt a great anxiety for Doctor Gordon, who sat shrugged up in his gray overcoat, with his gray grizzle of beard meeting the collar, and his forehead heavily corrugated over pent and gloomy eyes.

He was heartily glad when the service was over, when the casket had been lowered into the grave, when the village hearse had turned off into a street, the horse going at a sharp trot, and he and Doctor Gordon were left alone. He drove. Gordon sat hunched into a corner of the buggy, as he had sat in the corner of the hotel parlor. James hesitated about saying anything, but finally he spoke, he felt foolishly enough, although he meant the words to be comforting. "You did all you could to save his life," he said.

Gordon made no reply.

When they reached the house, Clemency's head disappeared from the window, where she had evidently been watching. She met them at the office door, with an odd, shocked, inquiring expression on her little face. James kissed her furtively, while Gordon's back was turned, as he divested himself of his gray coat.

"Dinner is nearly ready," Clemency said in an agitated voice.

"How is she?" asked Gordon, then before she had time to reply, he added almost roughly, "What on earth are you fretting about?"

"I am not fretting," Clemency answered in a weak little voice.

"There is nothing in all this for you to concern yourself with. Put it out of your head!"

"Yes, Uncle Tom."

"How is she?"

"She has been asleep all the afternoon."

"She has not had another attack?"

"No, Uncle Tom."

Then the dinner-bell rang.

To James's surprise, but everything surprised him now, Gordon seemed to recover his spirits. He ate heartily. He laughed and joked. After dinner he went upstairs to see Mrs. Ewing, and when he came down insisted that James should accompany him to the hotel for a game of euchre. James would have preferred remaining with Clemency, whose eyes were wistful, but Gordon hurried him away. They remained until nearly midnight in the parlor, where the funeral had taken place a short time before, playing euchre, telling stories, and drinking apple-jack. James noticed that the hotel man often cast an anxious and puzzled glance at Gordon. He began to fancy that what seemed mirth and jollity was the mere bravado of misery and a ghastly mask of real enjoyment. He was glad when Gordon made the move to leave. Georgie K. stood in the door watching the two men untie the horse and get into the buggy. "Take care of yourself, Doc," he hallooed, and there was real affection and concern in his voice.

Gordon drove now, and the mare, being on her homeward road, made good time. James helped Gordon unharness, as Aaron had gone to bed. His deep snores sounded through the stable from his room above. "It's a pity to wake up anything," Gordon said. "Guess well put the mare up ourselves." Now his voice was bitter again. Gordon had the key of the office door, and after locking the stable the two men entered. Gordon threw some wood on the fire. The lamp with its dangling prisms was burning. "Sit down a minute," Gordon said, "'I have something to tell you. I may as well get it off my mind now. It has got to come sometime."

James sat down and lit a cigar. He felt himself in a nervous tension. Gordon filled his pipe and lit it, then he began to speak in an odd, monotonous voice, as though he were reciting.

"That man's name was James Mendon. He was an Englishman. When I first began practice it was in the West. That man had a ranch near the little town where I lived with my sister Alice. Alice was a beautiful girl. We had lost our parents, and she kept house for me. The man was as handsome as a devil, and he had the devil's own way with women. God only knows what a good girl like my sister saw in him. He had a bad name, even out in that rough country. Horrible tales were circulated about his cruelty to animals for one thing. His cowboys deserted him and told stories. His very dog turned on him, and bit him. God knows how he was torturing the animal. I saw the scar on his hand when he lay on his deathbed. Well, however it was, my sister loved him and married him, and he treated her like a fiend. She died, and it was a merciful release. He deserted her three months before her death. Sold out all he had, and left her without a cent. She came back to me, and three months later Clemency was born."

Gordon paused and looked at James. "Yes," he said, "that man was Clemency's father."

He waited, but only for a second. The young man spoke, and his clear young voice rang out like a trumpet. "I never loved Clemency as I love her now," he said.

CHAPTER XI

Gordon smiled at James. "God bless you, boy!" he said. "What possible difference do you think that could make?" demanded James hotly. "Could that poor little girl help it?"

"Of course she could not, but some men might object, and with reason, to marrying a girl who came of such stock on her father's side."

"I am not one of those men."

"No, I don't think you are, but it is only my duty to put the case plainly before you. That man who was buried this afternoon was simply unspeakable. He was a monstrosity of perverted morality. I cannot even bring myself to tell you what I know of him. I cannot even bring myself to give you the least hint of what my poor young sister, Clemency's mother, suffered in her brief life with him. You may fear heredity—"

"Heredity, nothing! Don't I know Clemency?"

"I myself really think that you have nothing whatever to fear. Clemency is her mother's living and breathing image as far as looks go, and as far as I can judge in the innermost workings of her mind. I have not seen in her the slightest taint from her evil father, though God knows I have watched for it with horror as the years have passed. After she was born I smuggled her away by night, and gave out word that the child had died at the same time with the mother. There was a private funeral, and the casket was closed. I had hard work to carry it through successfully, for I was young in those days, and broken-hearted at losing my sister, but carry it through I did, and no one knew except a nurse. I trusted her, I was obliged to do so, and I fear that she has betrayed me. I established a practice in another town in another State, and there I met Clara. She has told me that she informed you of the fact that she was my wife, but not of our reasons for concealing it. Just before we were married I became practically certain that Clemency's father had gained in some way information that led him to suspect, if not to be absolutely certain, that his child had not died with his wife. I had a widowed sister, Mrs. Ewing, who lived in Iowa with her only daughter just about Clemency's age. Just before our marriage she decided to remove to England to live with some relatives of her deceased husband. They had considerable property, and she had very little. I begged her to go secretly, or rather to hint that she was going East to live with me, which she did. Nobody in the little Iowa village, so far as I knew, was aware of the fact that my sister and daughter had gone to England, and not East to live with me. Clara and I were married privately in an obscure little Western hamlet, and came East at once. We have lived in various localities, being driven from one to another by the danger of Clemency's father ascertaining the truth; and my wife has always been known as Mrs. Ewing, and Clemency as her daughter. It has been a life of constant watchfulness and deception, and I have been bound hand and foot. Even had Clemency's father not been so exceedingly careful that it would have been difficult to reach him by legal methods, there was the poor child to be considered, and the ignominy which would come upon her at the exposure of her father. I have done what I could. I am naturally a man who hates deception, and wishes above all things to lead a life with its windows open and shades up, but I have been forced into the very reverse. My life has been as closely shuttered and curtained as my house. I have been obliged to force my own wife to live after the same fashion. Now the cause for this secrecy is removed, but as far as she is concerned, the truth must still be concealed for Clemency's sake. It must not be known that that dead man was her father, and the very instant we let go one thread of the mystery the whole fabric will unravel. Poor Clara can never be acknowledged openly as my wife, the best and most patient wife a man ever had, and under a heavier sentence of death this moment than the utmost ingenuity of man could contrive." Gordon groaned, and let his head sink upon his hands.

"She told me some time ago that she was ill," James said pityingly.

"Ill? She has been upon the executioner's block for years. It is not illness; that is too tame a word for it. It is torture, prolonged as only the evil forces of Nature herself can prolong it."

Gordon rose and shook himself angrily. "I am keeping her now almost constantly under morphine," he said. "She has suffered more lately. The attacks have been more frequent. There has never been the slightest possibility of a surgical operation. From the very first it was utterly hopeless, and if it had been the dog there, I should have put a bullet through his head and considered myself a friend." Gordon gazed with miserable reflection at the dog. "I am glad that the *direct* cause of that man's death was not what it might have been," he said.

He shook himself again as a dog shakes off water. He laughed a miserable laugh. "Well," he said, "Clemency is free now. She can go her ways as she will. You see she resembled her mother so closely that I had to guard her from even the sight of her father. He would have known the truth at once. Clemency is free, but I have paid an awful price for her freedom and for your life. If I had not done what you doubtless know I did that night, you would have been shot, and it would have been a struggle between myself and her father, with the very good chance of my being killed, and Clara and the girl left defenseless. His revolver carried six deaths in it. It would all have depended upon the quickness of the dog, and I should have left too much hanging upon that."

"I don't see what else you could do," James said in a low voice. He was pale himself. He did not blame Gordon. He felt that he himself, in Gordon's place, would have done as he had done, and yet he felt as if faced close to a horror of murder and death, and he knew from the look upon the other man's countenance that it was the same with him.

"I saw no other way," Gordon said in a broken voice, "but—but I don't know whether I am a murderer or an executioner, and I never shall know. God help me! Well," he added with a sigh, "what is done, is done. Let us go to bed."

James said when they parted at his room door that he hoped Mrs. Ewing would have a comfortable night.

"Yes, she will," replied Gordon quietly. Then he gave the young man's hand a warm clasp. "God bless you!" he whispered. "If this had turned you against the child, it would have driven me madder than I am now. I love her as if she were my own. You and your loyalty are all I have to hold to."

"You can hold to that to the end," James returned with warmth, and he looked at Gordon as he might have looked at his own father.

Late as it was, he wrote that night to his own father and mother, telling them of his engagement to Clemency. There now can be no possible need for secrecy with regard to it. James, in spite of his vague sense of horror, felt an exhilaration at the thought that now all could be above board, that the shutters could be flung open. He felt as if an incubus had rolled from his mental consciousness. Clemency herself experienced something of the same feeling. She appeared at the breakfast-table the next morning with her hat. "Uncle says I may go with you on your rounds," she said to James. She beamed, and yet there was a troubled and puzzled expression on her pretty face. When she and James had started, and were moving swiftly along the country road, she said suddenly, "Will you tell me something?"

James hesitated.

"Will you?" she repeated.

"I can't promise, dear," he said.

"Why not?" she asked pettishly.

"Because it might be something which I ought not to tell you."

"You ought to tell me everything if—if—" she hesitated, and blushed.

"If what?" asked James tenderly.

She nestled up to him. "If you—feel toward me as you say you do."

"If. Oh, Clemency!"

"Then you ought to tell me. No, you needn't kiss me. I want you to tell me something. I don't want to be kissed."

"Well, what is that you want to know, dear?"

"Will you promise to tell me?"

"No, dear, I can't promise, but I will tell you if I am able without doing you harm."

"Who was that man who was buried yesterday, who had been hunting me so long, and frightening me and Uncle Tom, and why have I been compelled to stay housed as if I were a prisoner so much of my life?"

"Because you were in danger, dear, from the man."

"You are answering me in a circle." Clemency sat upright and looked at James, and the blue fire in her eyes glowed. "Who was the man?" she asked peremptorily.

"I can't tell you, dear."

"But you know."

"Yes."

"Why can't you tell me then?"

"Because it is not best."

Clemency shrugged her shoulders. "Why did he hunt me so?"

"I can't tell you, dear."

"But you know."

"I am not sure."

"But you think you know."

"Yes."

"Then tell me."

"I can't, dear."

"When will you tell me?"

"Never!"

Clemency looked at him, and again she blushed. "You will tell me after—we are—married. You will have to tell me everything then," she whispered.

James shook his head.

"Won't you then?"

"No, dear, I shall never tell you while I live."

Clemency made a sudden grasp at the reins. "Then I will never marry you," she said. "I will never marry you, if you keep things from me."

"I will never keep things from you that you ought to know, dear."

"I ought to know this!"

James remained silent. Clemency had brought the horse to a full stop. "Won't you ever tell me?" she asked.

"No, never! dear."

"Then let me get out. This is Annie Lipton's street. I am going to see her. I have not seen her for a long time. I will walk home. It is safe enough now. You can tell me that much?"

"Yes, it is, but Clemency, dear."

"I am not Clemency, dear. I am not going to marry you. You say you wrote your father and mother last night that we were going to get married. Well, you can just write again and tell them we are not. No, you need not try to stop me. I will get out. Good-by! I shall not be home to luncheon. I shall stay with Annie. I like her very much better than I like you."

With that Clemency had slipped out of the buggy and hurried up a street without looking back. James drove on. He felt disturbed, but not seriously so. It was impossible to take Clemency's anger as a real thing. It was so whimsical and childish. He had counted upon his long morning with her, but he went on with a little smile on his face.

He was half inclined to think, so slightly did he estimate Clemency's anger, that she would not keep her word, and would be home for luncheon. But when he returned she was not there, and she had not come when the bell rang.

"Why, where is Clemency?" Gordon said, when they entered the dining-room.

"She insisted upon stopping to see her friend Miss Lipton," said James. "She said that she might not be home to lunch." Emma gave one of her sharp, baffled glances at him, then, having served the two men, she tossed her head and went out. Nobody knew how much she wished to listen at the kitchen door, but she was above such a course.

"Clemency and I had a bit of a tiff," James explained to Gordon. "She seemed vexed because I would not tell her what you told me last night. She is curious to know more about—that man."

"She must not know," Gordon said quickly. "Never mind if she does seem a little vexed. She will get over it. I know Clemency. She is like her mother. The power of sustained indignation against one she loves is not in the child, and she must not know. It would be a dreadful thing for her to know. I myself cannot have it. It is enough of a horror as it is, but to have that child look at me, and think—" Gordon broke off abruptly.

"She will never know through me," James said, "and I think with you that her resentment will not last."

"She will be home this afternoon," said Gordon, "and the walk will do her good."

But the two returned from their afternoon calls, and still Clemency had not returned. Emma met them at the door. "Mrs. Ewing says she is worried about Miss Clemency," she said. Gordon ran upstairs. When he came down he joined James in the office. "I have pacified Clara," he said, "but suppose you jump into the buggy, Aaron has not unharnessed yet, and drive over to Annie Lipton's for her. It is growing colder, and Clemency has not been outdoors much lately, and she has rather a delicate throat. It is time now that she was home."

James smiled. "Suppose she will not come with me?" he suggested.

"Nonsense," said Gordon. "She will be only too glad if you meet her half-way. She will come. Tell her I said that she must."

"All right," replied James.

He went out, got into the buggy, and drove along rapidly. He had the team, and the horses were still quite fresh, as they had not been long distances that day. There was a vague fear in the young man's mind, although he tried to dispel it by the force of argument.

"What has the girl to fear now?" his reason kept dinning in his ears, but, in spite of himself, something else, which seemed to him unreason, made him anxious. When he reached Annie Lipton's home, a fine old house, overhung with a delicate tracery of withered vines, he saw Annie's pretty head at a front window. She opened the door before he had time to ring the bell, and she looked with alarmed questioning at him.

"I have come for Miss Ewing, her uncle—" James began, but Annie interrupted him, her face paling perceptibly. "Clemency," she said; "why, she left here directly after lunch. She said she must go. She felt anxious about her mother, and did not want to leave her any longer. Hasn't she come home yet?"

"No," said James.

"And you didn't meet her? You must have met her."

"No."

The two stood staring at each other. A delicate old face peeped out of the door at the right of the halls. It was like Annie's, only dimmed by age, and shaded by two leaf-like folds of gray hair as smooth as silver. "Oh, mother, Clemency has not got home!" Annie cried. "Dr. Elliot, this is my mother. Mother, Clemency has not got home. What do you think has happened?"

The lady came out in the hall. She had a quiet serenity of manner, but her soft eyes looked anxious. "Could she have stopped anywhere, dear?" she said.

"You know, mother, there is not a single house between here and her own where Clemency ever stops," said Annie. She was trembling all over.

James made a movement to go. "What are you going to do?" cried Annie.

"Stop at every house between here and Doctor Gordon's, and ask if the people have seen her," replied James.

Then he ran back to the buggy, and heard as he went a little nervous call from Annie, "Oh, let us know if—"

"I will let you know when I find her, Miss Lipton," he called back as he gathered up the lines. He kept his word. He did stop at every house, and at every one all knowledge of the girl was disclaimed. There were not many houses, the road being a lonely one. He was met mostly by women who seemed at once to share his anxiety. One woman especially asked very carefully for a description of Clemency, and he gave a minute one. "You say her mother is ill, too," said the woman. She was elderly, but still pretty. She had kept her tints of youth as some withered flowers do, and there seemed still to cling to her the atmosphere of youth, as fragrance clings to dry rose leaves. She was dressed in rather a superior fashion to most of the countrywomen, in soft lavender cashmere which fitted her slight, tall figure admirably. James had a glimpse behind her of a pretty interior: a room with windows full of blooming plants, of easy-chairs and many cushioned sofas, beside book-cases. The woman looked, so he thought, like one who had some private anxiety of her own. She kept peering up and down the road, as they talked, as though she, too, were on the watch for some one. She promised James to keep a lookout for the missing girl. "Poor little thing," she murmured. There was something in her face as she said that, a slight phase of amusement, which caused James to stare keenly at her, but it had passed, and her whole face denoted the utmost candor and concern.

When James reached home he had a forlorn hope that he should find Clemency there; that from a spirit of mischief she had taken some cross track over the fields to elude him. But when Aaron met him in the drive, and he saw the man's frightened stare, he knew that she had not come. It was unnecessary to ask, but ask he did. "She has not come?"

"No, Doctor Elliot," replied Aaron. He did not even chew. He tied the horses, and followed James into the office, with his jaws stiff. Gordon stood up when James entered, and looked past him for Clemency. "She was not there?" he almost shouted.

"She left the Liptons at two o'clock, and I have stopped at every house on my way, and no one has seen her."

"Oh, my God!" said Gordon, with a dazed look at James.

"What do you think?" asked James.

"I don't know what to think. I am utterly at a loss now. I supposed she was entirely safe. There are almost no tramps at this season, and in broad daylight. At two, you said? It is almost six. I don't know what to do. What will come next? I must tell Clara something before I do anything else."

Gordon rushed out of the office, and they heard his heavy tread on the stairs. Aaron stared at James, and still he did not chew.

"It's almost dark," he said with a low drawl.

"Yes."

"We've got to take lanterns, and hunt along the road and

fields."

"Yes, we have."

The dog, which had been asleep, got up, and came over to James, and laid his white head on his knee. "We can take him," Aaron said. "Sometimes dogs have more sense than us."

"That is so," said James. He felt himself in an agony of helplessness. He simply did not know what to do. He had sunk into a chair and his head fairly rung. It seemed to him incredible that the girl had disappeared a second time. A queer sense of unreality made him feel faint.

Gordon reëntered the room. "I have told Clara that you have come back, and that Clemency is to stay all night with Annie Lipton," he said. Then he, too, stood staring helplessly. Emma had come into the room, and now she spoke angrily to the three dazed men. "Git the lanterns lit, for goodness' sake," said she, "and hunt and do something. I'm goin' to git her supper, and I'll keep her pacified." Emma gave a jerk with a sharp elbow toward Mrs. Ewing's room. "For goodness' sake, if you don't know yet where she has went, why don't you do somethin'?" she demanded. The men went before her sharp command like dust before her broom. "Keep as still as you can," ordered Emma as they went out. "*She* mustn't, git to worryin' before she comes home."

For the next two hours Gordon, James, and Aaron searched. They walked, each going his separate way into the fields and woods on the road, having agreed upon a signal when the girl should be found. The signal was to be a pistol shot. James went first to the wood, where he had found Clemency on her former disappearance. He searched in every shadow, throwing the gleam of his lantern into little dark nests of last year's ferns, and hollows where last year's leaves had swirled together to die, but no Clemency. At last, wearied and heart-sick, he came out on the road. The moon was just up, a full moon, and the road lay stretched before him like a silver ribbon covered with the hoar-frost. He gazed down it hopelessly, and saw a little dark figure running toward him. He was incredulous, but he called, "Clemency!"

A glad little cry answered him. He himself ran forward, and the girl was in his arms, sobbing and trembling as if her heart would break.

"What has happened? What has happened, darling?" James cried in an agony. "Are you hurt? What has happened?"

"Something very strange has happened, but I am not hurt," sobbed Clemency. James remembered the signal. "Wait a second, dear," he said; "your uncle and Aaron are searching, and I promised to fire the pistol if I found you." James fired his pistol in the air six times. Then he returned to Clemency, who was leaning against a tree. "How I wish we had driven here!" James said tenderly.

"I can walk, if you help me," Clemency sobbed, leaning against him. "Oh, I am so sorry I acted so this morning. I got punished for it. I haven't been hurt, nobody has been anything but kind to me, but I have been dreadfully frightened."

Gordon and Aaron came running up. "Where have you been, Clemency?" Gordon demanded in a harsh voice. "Another time you must do as you are told. You are too old to behave like a child, and put us all in such a fright."

Clemency left James, and ran to her uncle, and clung to him sobbing hysterically. "Oh, Uncle Tom, don't scold me," she whimpered.

"Are you hurt? What has happened?"

"I am not hurt a bit," sobbed Clemency.

Gordon put his arm around her. "Well," he said, "as long as you are safe keep your story until we get home. Elliot, take her other arm. She is almost too used up to walk. Now stop crying, Clemency."

When they were home, in the office, Clemency told her story, which was a strange one. She had been on her way home from Annie Lipton's, and had reached a certain house, when the door opened and a woman stood there calling her. She described the woman and the house, and James gave a start. "That must be the same woman whom I saw," he exclaimed.

"She was a woman I had never seen," said Clemency. "I think she had only lived there a very short time."

Gordon nodded gloomily. "I know who she is, I fear," he said. "Strange that I did not suspect."

"She looked very kind and pleasant," said Clemency, "and I thought she wanted something and there was no harm, but when I reached her the first thing I knew she had hold of me, and her hands were like iron clamps. She put one over my mouth, and held me with the other, and pulled me into the house and locked the door. Then she made me go into a little dark room in the middle of the house and she locked me in. She told me if I screamed nobody would hear me, but she did speak kindly. She was very kind. Once she even kissed me, although I did not want her to. She brought a lamp in, and made me lie down on a couch in the room and drink a glass of wine. She told me not to be afraid, nobody would hurt me. She seemed to me to be always listening, and every now and then she went out, but she always locked the door behind her. When she came back she would look terribly worried. About half an hour ago she went out, and when she came back brought a tray with tea and bread and cold chicken for me. I told her I would starve before I ate anything while she kept me there. She did not seem to pay much attention, she looked so dreadfully worried. She sat down and looked at me. Finally, she said, as if she were afraid to hear her own voice, 'Has any accident happened near here lately that you have heard of?' I told her about the man that fell down in our drive and died of erysipelas. I did not tell her anything else. All at once she almost fell in a faint. Then she stood up, and she looked as if she were dead. She told me to stay where I was just fifteen minutes, then I might go, but I must not stir before. Then she kissed me again, and her lips were like ice. She went out, and I knew the door was not locked, but I was afraid to stir. I could hear her running about. Then I heard the outer door slam, and I looked at my watch, and it was fifteen minutes. Then I ran out and up the road as fast as I could. Just before I saw Doctor Elliot the New York train passed. I heard it. I think she was hurrying to catch that."

Gordon nodded.

"Oh, Uncle Tom, who was she, and why did she lock me up?" asked Clemency.

"Clemency," said Gordon, in a sterner voice than Clemency had ever heard him use toward her, "never speak, never think, of that woman or that man again. Now go out and eat your dinner."

CHAPTER XII

Clemency was so worn out that Doctor Gordon insisted upon her going to bed directly after dinner, and he and James had a solitary evening in the office, with the exception of Gordon's frequent absence in his wife's room. Each time when he returned he looked more gloomy. "I have increased the morphine almost as much as I dare," he said, coming into the office about ten. He sat down and lit his pipe. James laid down the evening paper which he had been reading. "Is she asleep now?" he asked.

"Yes. By the way, Elliot, have you guessed who that woman was who kidnapped Clemency?"

James hesitated. "I don't fairly know whether I am right, but I have guessed," he replied.

"Who?"

"The nurse."

"You are right. It was the nurse. That man had won her over, and set her up housekeeping in Westover. He had been staying at the hotel there before he came here. He was her lover, of course, although he was too circumspect not to guard the secret. She has been living in that house for the last three months under the name of Mrs. Wood, a widow. The former occupants went away last summer, Aaron has been telling me. He said that once he himself saw the man enter the house, and he had seen the woman on the street. She had made herself quite popular in Westover. It was no part of that man's policy to keep his vice behind locked doors. Locks themselves are the best witness against evil. She attended the Dutch Reformed Church regularly. She was present at all the church suppers, and everybody has called on her in Westover. Now I think she has fled, half-crazed with grief over the death of her lover, and afraid of some sort of exposure. Unless I miss my guess, there will be a furor around here shortly over her disappearance. She was not a bad woman as I remember her, and she was attractive, with a kindly disposition. But he had his way always with women, and I suppose she thought she was doing him a service by kidnapping poor little Clemency. I am sorry for her. I hope she did not go away penniless, but she has her nursing to fall back upon. She was a good nurse. That makes me think. I must see if Mrs. Blair cannot come here tomorrow. Clara must have somebody beside Clemency and Emma. I should prefer a trained nurse, and this woman is simply the self-taught village sort, but Clara prefers her. She shrinks at the very mention of a trained nurse. Of course, it is unreasonable, but the poor soul has always had an awful dread of hospitals and a possible operation, and I believe that in some way she thinks a trained nurse one of a dreadful trinity. She must be humored, of course. The result cannot be changed."

"You have no hope, then?" James said in a low voice.

"I have had no more from the outset than if she had been already dead," said Gordon.

James said nothing. An enormous pity for the other man was within him. He thought of Clemency, and he seemed to undergo the same pangs. He felt such a terrible understanding of the other's suffering that it passed the bounds of sympathy. It became almost experience. His young face took on the same expression of dull misery as Gordon's. Presently Gordon glanced at him, and spoke with a ring of gratitude and affection in his tired voice.

"You are a good fellow, Elliot," he said, "and you are the one ray of comfort I have. I am glad that I have you to leave poor little Clemency with."

James looked at him with sudden alarm. "You are not ill?" he said.

"No, but there is an end to everybody's rope, and sometimes I think I am about at the end of mine. I don't know. Anyway, it is a comfort to me to think that Clemency has you in case anything should happen to me."

"She has me as long as I live," James said fervently. Red overspread his young face, his eyes glistened. Again the great pity and understanding with regard to the other man came over him, and a feeling for Clemency which he had never before had: a feeling greater than love itself, the very angel of love, divinest pity and protection, for all womanhood, which was exemplified for himself in this one girl. His heart ached, as if it were Clemency's upstairs, lying miserably asleep under the influence of the drug, which alone could protect her from indescribable pain. His mind projected itself into the future, and realized the possibility of such suffering for her, and for himself. The honey-sting of pain, which love has, stung him sharply.

Gordon seemed to divine his thoughts. "God grant that you may never have to undergo what I am undergoing, boy," he said. Then he added, "It was in poor Clara's blood, her mother before her died the same way. Clemency comes, on her mother's side at least, of a healthy race, morally and physically, although the nervous system is oversensitive. If my poor sister had been happy, she would have been alive today. And as far as I know of the other side, there was perfect physical health, although he had that abnormal lack of moral sense that led one to dream of possession. Did you notice how much less evil he looked when he was dead, even with that frightfully disfigured face?"

"Yes."

"There are strange things in this world," said Gordon with gloomy reflection, "or else simple things which we are strange not to believe. Sometimes I think people will have to take to the Bible again in that literal sense in which so many are now inclined to disregard it. Well, Elliot, I honestly feel that you have nothing to fear in taking poor little Clemency. I should tell you if I thought otherwise. She will make you happy, and I can think of no reason to warn you concerning any possible lapses, in either her physical or her moral health, and I have had her in my charge since she first drew the breath of life. Come, my son, it is late, and we have a great deal to do tomorrow. This awful business has made me neglect patients. I have to see Clara again, and get what rest I can." Gordon looked older and wearier than James had ever seen him, as he bade him good-night, old and weary as he had often seen him look. A sudden alarm for Gordon himself came over him. He wondered, after he had entered, his room, if he were not strained past endurance. He recalled his own father's healthy, ruddy face, and Gordon was no older.

He lay awake a while thinking anxiously of Gordon, then his own happy future blazoned itself before him, and he dreamed awake, and dreamed asleep, of himself and Clemency, in that future, whose golden vistas had no end, so far as his young eyes could see. The sense of relief from anxiety over the girl was so intense that it was in itself a delight. Clemency herself felt it. The next morning at breakfast she looked radiant. Gordon had assured her the sick woman had rested quietly, and told her that Mrs. Blair was coming.

"Today I can go where I choose," Clemency exclaimed gayly.

"Not until afternoon," replied Gordon, then he relented at her look of disappointment, and suggested that she go with Elliot to make his calls, while he went with Aaron and the team. It was a beautiful morning; spring seemed to have arrived. Everywhere was the plash of running water, now and then came distant flutings of birds. "I know that was a bluebird," Clemency said happily. "I feel sure mother will get well now. It seems wicked to be glad that the man is dead, especially on such a morning, but I wonder if it is, when he would have spoiled the morning."

"Don't think about it, anyway!" James said.

"I try not to."

"You must not!"

"I know why Uncle Tom did not want me to go out alone this morning," Clemency said, with one of her quick wise looks, cocking her head like a bird.

"Why?"

"He wanted to make sure that that woman has really gone."

"Clemency, you must not mention that man or woman to me again," said James.

"I am not married to you yet," Clemency said, pouting.

"That makes no difference, you must promise."

"Well, then, I will. I am so happy this morning, that I will promise anything."

James looked about to be sure nobody was in sight before he kissed the little radiant face.

"I won't speak of them again, but I am right," Clemency said with a little toss and blush, and it proved that she was.

At luncheon Doctor Gordon told Clemency that she could go wherever she liked. She gave a little glance at James, and said gayly, "All right, Uncle Tom."

That afternoon Gordon and James made some calls in company, driving far into the hills. They had hardly started before Gordon said abruptly, "Well, the woman is gone, and there is a wild excitement in Westover over her disappearance. I believe they are about to drag the pond. A man who knew her well by sight declares that she boarded that New York train, but the people will not give up the theory that she has been murdered for her jewelry. By the way, I think I need not worry over her immediate necessities. It seems that she had worn a quantity of very valuable jewels. Of course her going without any baggage except a suit-case, and leaving behind the greater part of her wardrobe, does look singular. But it seems that the house was rented furnished, and I fancy she lived always in light marching orders, and probably carried the most valuable of her possessions upon her person and in her suit-case. Well, I am thankful she has decamped."

"You don't fear her returning?" asked James with some anxiety.

"No, I have no fear of that. She is probably broken-hearted over the death of that man. She is not of the sort to kidnap on her own account. It was only for him. Clemency has nothing more to fear."

"I am thankful."

"You can well believe that I am, when I tell you that this afternoon I am absolutely sure, for the first time in years, that the girl is safe to come and go as she pleases. I have had hideous uncertainty as well as hideous certainty to cope with. Now it is down to the hideous certainty. That is bad enough, but fate on an open field is less unmanning than fate in ambush. I have long known to a nicety the fate in the field." Gordon hesitated a second, then he said abruptly, with his face turned from his companion, in a rough voice, "Clara can't last many days."

James made an exclamation.

"She has gone down hill rapidly during the last two days," said Gordon. "I have been increasing the morphine. It can't last long." Gordon ended the sentence with a hoarse sob.

"I can't say anything," James faltered after a second, "but you know—"

"Yes, I know," Gordon said. "You are as sorry as any one can be who is not, so to speak, the hero, or rather the coward, of the tragedy. Yes, I know. I'm obliged to you, Elliot, but all of us have to face death, whether it is our own or the death of another dearer than ourselves, alone. A soul is a horribly lonely thing in the worst places of life."

"Have you told Clemency?"

"No, I have put it off until the last minute. What good can it do? She knows that Clara is very ill, but she does not know, she has never known, the character of the illness. Sometimes I have a curious feeling that instinct has asserted itself, and that Clemency, fond as she is of my wife, has not exactly the affection which she would have had for her own mother."

"I don't think she knows any difference at all," James said. "I think the poor little girl will about break her heart."

"I did not mean to underestimate Clemency's affection," said

Gordon, "but what I say is true. The girl herself will never know it, and, you may not believe it, but she will not suffer as she would suffer if Clara were her own mother. These ties of the blood are queer things, nothing can quite take their place. If Clemency had died first Clara would have been indignant at the suggestion, but she herself would not have mourned as she would mourn for her own daughter. I must touch up the horses a bit. I want to get home. I may not be able to go out again tonight. Last night I was up until dawn with Clara." Gordon touched the horses with a slight flicker of the whip. He held the lines taut as they sprang forward. His face was set ahead. James glancing at him had a realization of the awful loneliness of the other man by his side. He seemed to comprehend the vastness of the isolation of a grief which concerns one, and one only, more than any other. Gordon had the expression of a wanderer upon a desert or a frozen waste. Illimitable distances of solitude seemed reflected in his gloomy eyes.

James did not attempt to talk to him. It seemed like mockery, this effort to approach with sympathy this set-apart man, who was unapproachable.

That night Gordon's wife was much worse. Gordon came down to James's room about two o'clock. James had been awake for some time listening to the sounds of suffering overhead, and he had lit his lamp and dressed, thinking that he might be needed. Gordon stood in the doorway almost reeling. He made an effort before he spoke.

"Come into my office, will you?" he said.

James at once followed him. Going through the hall the sounds of agony became more distinct. When they entered the office Gordon fairly slammed the door, then he turned to Elliot with a savage expression. "Hear that," he said, as if he were accusing the other man. "Hear that, I say! The last hypodermic has not taken effect yet, and her heart is weak. If I give her more—"

He stopped, staring at James, his face worked like a child's. Then suddenly an almost idiotic expression came over it, the utter numbness of grief. Then it passed away. Again he looked intelligently into the young man's eyes. "If I don't give her more," he gasped out, "if I don't, this may last hours. If I do—"

The two men stood staring at each other. James thought of Clemency. "Has Clemency been in to see her?" he asked.

"Yes, she heard, and came in. I sent her out. She is in her own room now; Emma is with her." Suddenly Gordon gave a look of despairing appeal at James. "I—wish you would go up and see Clara," he whispered.

James knew what he meant. He hesitated.

"Go, and send Mrs. Blair down here," said Gordon. "Tell her I want to see her."

"Well," said James slowly.

The two men did not look at each other again. Gordon sank into his chair. James went out of the room and upstairs. He knocked on the door of the sick-room, and Mrs. Blair, the village nurse, answered his knock. She was a large woman in a voluminous wrapper. Her face had a settled expression of gravity, almost of sternness. She looked at James. The screams from the writhing mass of agony in the bed did not appear to be moving her, whereas she in reality was herself screwed to such a pitch of mental torture of pity that she was scarcely able to move. She was rigid.

"Doctor Gordon sent me," whispered James. "He wished me to see her. He asked me to say to you that he would like to see you for a minute in the office."

The woman did not move for a second. Then she whispered close to James's ear, "*It is on the bureau.*"

James nodded. They passed each other. James entered the room and closed the door. A lamp was burning on a table with a screen before it. The bed was in shadow. The screams never ceased. They were not human. James could not realize that the beautiful woman whom he had known was making such sounds. They sounded like the shrieks of an animal. All the soul seemed gone from them.

James approached the bed. There was a roll of dark eyes at him. Then a voice ghastly beyond description, like the snarl of a hungry beast, came from between the straight white lips. "More, more! Give me more! Be quick!"

James hesitated.

"Quick, quick!" demanded the voice.

James crossed the room to the dresser. The sick woman now interspersed her screams with the word "quick!"

James filled a hypodermic syringe from a glass on the bureau and approached the bed again. He bared a shuddering arm and inserted the instrument quickly. "Now try and be quiet," he said. "You will go to sleep."

Then he went out of the room. The screams had ceased. As James approached the stair another door opened, and Clemency in a wrapper looked out. She was very pale, her eyes were distended with fear, and her mouth was trembling. "How is she?" she whispered.

"Better, dear. Go back in your room and lie down. We are doing all we can."

When James entered the office Gordon and Mrs. Blair turned with one accord, and fixed horribly searching eyes upon his face. He sat down beside the table, and mechanically lit a cigar.

"How did she seem?" Gordon asked almost inaudibly.

"Better."

"Was she quiet?"

"Yes."

Gordon gave a long sigh. His face was deadly white. He leaned back in his chair, and both James and the nurse sprang. They thought he had fainted. While James felt his pulse Mrs. Blair got some brandy. Gordon swallowed the brandy, and raised his head.

"It is nothing," he said in a harsh voice. "You had better go back to her, Mrs. Blair."

A look of strange dread came over the woman's grave face.

"I will be there directly," said Gordon.

Mrs. Blair went out. She left the door ajar. The house was so still that one could seem to hear the silence. There was something terrible about it after the turmoil of sound. Then the silence was broken. A scream more terrible than ever pierced it like a sword. Another came. Gordon sprang up and faced James. The young man's eyes fell before the look of fierce questioning in Gordon's.

"I could not," he gasped. "Oh, Doctor Gordon, I could not! Instead of that I used water. I thought perhaps her mind being convinced that it was morphine, she might—"

"Mind!" shouted Gordon. "Mind, how much do you suppose the poor, tortured thing has to bring to bear upon this? I tell you she is being eaten alive. There is no other word for it. Gnawed, and worried, and eaten alive." Gordon ran out of the room.

James closed the door. The dog, who had been asleep beside the fire, started up, came over to James, laid his white head on his knee and whimpered, with an appealing look in his brown eyes, which were turned toward the young man's face. Almost immediately Mrs. Blair entered the room. She was very pale. "Doctor

Gordon sent me down for the brandy," she said abruptly. She went to the table on which the brandy flask stood, but she seemed in no hurry to take it.

"How is she?" asked James.

"I think she is a little quieter." The nurse stood staring at the fire for a second longer. Then she took the brandy flask and went out with a soft, but jarring, tread.

Doctor Gordon must have passed her on the stairs, for he returned almost directly after she had left, and stood with his back to James, fussing over some bottles on the shelves opposite the fireplace. He stood there for some five minutes. James glancing over his shoulder saw that he was trembling in a strange rigid fashion, but he seemed intent upon the bottles. The house was very still again. Gordon at last seemed to have finished whatever he was doing with the bottles. He left them and sat down in his chair. The dog left James and went to him, but Gordon pushed him away roughly. Then Gordon spoke to James without turning his face in his direction. "I wish you would go upstairs," he said hoarsely. "Mrs. Blair is alone, and I—I am about done too."

James obeyed without a word. When he reached the head of the stairs he felt a sudden draught of cold wind. Mrs. Blair came out of the sick-room, closing the door behind her. Her face looked as stern as fate itself. James knew what had happened the moment he saw her.

James began to speak stammeringly, but she stopped him. "Call Doctor Gordon," she said shortly. "She is dead."

CHAPTER XIII

About two weeks after the death of Doctor Gordon's wife James went to the post office before beginning his round of calls. Lately nearly all the practice had devolved upon him. Gordon seemed sunken in a gloomy apathy, from which he could rouse himself only for the most urgent necessities. Once aroused he was fully himself, but for the most part he sat in his office smoking or seemingly half-asleep. Once in a while a very sick patient acted upon him as a momentary stimulus, but Alton was unusually healthy just then. After an open and, for the most part, snowless winter, which had occasioned much sickness, the spring brought frost and light falls of snow, which seemed to give new life to people in spite of unseasonableness. James had had little difficulty in attending to most of the practice, although he was necessarily away from home the greater part of the time. However, he often took Clemency with him, and she would sit well wrapped up in the buggy reading a book while he made calls. Then there were the long drives over solitary roads, which, though rough, causing the wheels to jolt heavily in deep ridges of frozen soil, or sink into the red mud almost to the hubs, as the case might be, seemed like roads of Paradise to the young man. Although he himself grieved for Gordon's wife, and Gordon himself filled him with covert anxiety, yet he was young and the girl was young, and they were both released from a miserable sense of insecurity and mystery, which had irritated and saddened them; their thoughts now turned toward their own springtime, as naturally and innocently as flowers bloom. There was grief, and the shadow of trouble, but of past trouble; their eyes looked upon life and love and joy instead of death, as helplessly as a flower looks toward the sun. They were happy, although half-ashamed of their happiness; but, after all, perhaps, being happy after bereavement and trouble means simply that the soul has turned to God for consolation.

James's face was beaming with his joyful thoughts as he drew up before the village store, got out of the buggy, and tied the horse. When he entered he said "good morning!" in a sort of general fashion. There were many men lounging about. The morning mail had been distributed, and although Alton people got very few letters, still there was a wide interest in the post office, a little boxed-off space in a corner of the store. The store-keeper, Henry Graves, was the postmaster. He felt the importance of his position. When he sorted and distributed the mail from the limp leather bag, he realized himself as an official of a great republic. He loved to proudly ignore, and not even seem to see, the interested and gaping faces watching the boxes. Doctor Gordon's box was an object of especial interest. Indeed, that was the only one to be depended upon to contain something when the two mails per day arrived. Gordon, moreover, took the only New York paper which reached the little hamlet. Alton had no paper of its own. The nearest was printed in Stanbridge. One man, the Presbyterian minister, subscribed to the Stanbridge paper, and paid for it in farm produce. He had a little farm, and tilled the soil when he was not saving souls. The Stanbridge paper had arrived the night before, and the minister had been good enough to impart some of its contents to the curious throng in the store. He was accustomed to do so. Likewise Gordon, when he was not too hurried, would open his New York paper, and read the most startling "headers" to a wide-eyed audience. This morning the paper was in the box as usual, with a number of letters. The men pressed in a suggestive way around James, as he took the parcel from the postmaster. There were no lock-boxes. James hesitated a moment. He had not much time, but he was good-natured, and the eager hunger in the men's eyes appealed to him. There was something pathetic about this outreaching for intelligence of their kind, and its progress or otherwise, among these plodding folk, who had so to count their pence that a newspaper was an unheard-of luxury to them.

James opened the paper and glanced over the headlines on the first page. Now, had he looked, he might have seen something sinister and malicious in the curious eyes, but he was so dazed by the very first thing he saw as to be for the moment oblivious to anything else. On the right of the first page was the headline: "Strange dual life of a prominent physician in Alton, New Jersey. Doctor Thomas B. Gordon has lived with his wife for years, and called her his widowed sister, Mrs. Clara Ewing. Upon her death, a few days since, he revealed the secret. Will give no reasons for this strange conduct, simply states that he was justified, even compelled, by circumstances." Then followed a caricature portrait of Gordon, a photograph of the house, one of the village church, and the cemetery and Gordon's wife's grave, with various surmises and comments, enough to fill the column. James paled as he read. He had not known of Gordon's action in telling that the dead woman was his wife. He looked around in a bewildered fashion, and met the hungry eyes. One small, mean face of a small man peered around his shoulder gloatingly. "Some news this mornin'?" he observed, with a smack of the lips, as if he tasted sweets.

Then James arose to the occasion. He faced them all and smiled coolly. "Yes," he replied; "you mean about Doctor Gordon?"

There was a murmur of assent.

James read the article from beginning to end. "I suppose it is news to you," he said, when he had finished. He looked at them all with a superior air. He looked older and more manly than when he had first come in their midst. He *was* older and more manly, and he was superior. The men recognized it, not sullenly nor defiantly, but with the unquestioning attitude of the New Jerseyman when he is really below the scale in birth and education. Still their faces all expressed malicious cunning and cruel curiosity, which they hesitated to put into words. They knew that Elliot was to marry Gordon's niece; they were overawed by both men, but they were afraid of Gordon.

Still Jim Goodman found courage of his meanness and smallness and spoke. "It seems a strange thing," he said, "that Doctor Gordon should hev came and went here for years, and all of us thinkin' his wife were his sister when she were not."

"Well, what of it?" asked James.

The men stared at one another.

"What of it?" repeated James. "I don't suppose there is anything criminal in a man's calling his wife by his sister's name. Doctor Gordon has a sister named Ewing."

Again the men stared at one another, and Jim Goodman was the only one who had the miserable courage to speak. "S'pose him an' her were married," he said, in a thin voice like the squeal of a fox.

"Which of you wants to be knocked down can make a statement to the contrary," thundered James. "Is that what you make of it?"

Goodman shuffled from one foot to the other. Men nudged shoulders, Goodman spoke. "Nobody never knows what is true or ain't true in them newspapers," he observed, and there was a note of alarm in his voice.

"I did not read a thing in the whole column which even

implied such a thing as you intimated," James said hotly. "Don't put it off on the newspapers!"

Then another man spoke, a farmer, tall, dry, lank, and impervious. He was a man about whom were ill-reports. His wife had died some years before, and he had a housekeeper, a florid, blonde creature, dressed with dingy showiness, of whom people spoke with covert laughs. "All we want to know is why Doctor Gordon has never said that her was his wife, and not his sister," he said in a defiant nasal voice.

The malignant Jim Goodman saw his chance. He jumped upon it like a spider. "That's so," he said. "Why didn't he say she was his housekeeper?" There was a shout of coarse laughter. The farmer gave a hateful look at Goodman and puffed at a rank pipe.

James was furious, but he saw the necessity of a statement of some kind, and his wits leaped to action. "Well," he said, "suppose there was a question of money."

The crowd pressed closer and gaped.

"Money!" said Goodman.

"Yes, money," pursued James recklessly. "Did you never hear of people being opposed to marriages, rich people I mean, and threatening to disinherit a woman if she married the man they did not pick out for her?"

"Was that it?" asked Goodman.

"I am not saying that it was or was not. I am not going to discuss Doctor Gordon's secrets with you. It's none of your business, and none of my business. All I am saying is this, suppose there had been a girl years ago with a very rich bachelor brother. Suppose the brother had been jilted by a girl, and hated the whole lot of women like poison, and had no idea of getting married himself, and his sister would be his only heiress, and he had set his foot down that she should not marry Doc—the man she had set her heart upon. Suppose he went to—well, the South Sea Islands, for the rest of his life, to get out of sight and sound of women like the one who had jilted him, told his sister before he went that if she married the man she wanted he would make a will and leave his money away from her, build an hospital or a library or something, suppose she hit upon the plan of marrying the man she wanted, and keeping it quiet."

"Was that it?"

"Didn't I tell you that I would not say whether it was or not? I only say suppose that was the case. Doctor Gordon has a married sister by the name of Ewing living in foreign parts. You can see for yourself how easy it might have been."

"What about the girl?" asked Goodman in a dry voice.

James flushed angrily. "That is nobody's business," said he. "She is Doctor Gordon's niece."

Goodman was unabashed. "How does it happen her name is Ewing?" he asked.

"Couldn't it possibly have happened that two sisters of Doctor Gordon's married two brothers?" James cried. He elbowed his way out. When he was in the buggy driving home, he began to realize how the fairy tale which he had related in the store would not in the least impose upon Clemency, how she would almost inevitably hear of the statements in the papers. He wondered more and more that Gordon should have divulged a secret which he had kept so fiercely for so long.

When he reached home he went at once into the office, and gave Gordon his mail and the New York paper. Gordon glanced at it, then at James. "Have you seen this?" he asked.

James nodded.

"I suppose you think me most inconsistent," said Gordon gloomily, "but the truth is I kept the secret while Clara was alive, though I found I could not, oh, God, I could not after she was dead and gone! I had not realized what that would mean: to never acknowledge her as my wife, dead or alive. I found that when it came to the death certificate, and the notice in the paper, and the erection of a stone to her memory, that I could not keep up the deception, no matter what the consequence. My God, Elliot, I cannot commit sacrilege against the dead! Dead, she must have her due. I anticipated this. There was something last night in the *Stanbridge Record*, and yesterday, while you were out three reporters from New York came. I told them that I had done what I had for good and sufficient reasons, which were not dishonorable to myself or to others, and beyond that I would say nothing. I suppose the poor fellows had to tax their imaginations to fill their columns. I don't know what the result will be with regard to Clemency, but I could not help it." There was something painfully appealing in Gordon's look and manner. He seemed so broken that James was alarmed. He said everything that he was able to say to soothe him, commended the course which he had taken, and told him what he had said at the store, without repeating the insinuations which had led him to fabricate such a tale. Gordon smiled bitterly. "All your fellowmen want of you is food for their animal appetites or their mental," he said. "They must have meat and drink for their stomachs, as well as for their curiosity and malice. I have lived here all these years, and labored for them for mighty poor recompense, and sometimes for none at all, and I'll warrant that today I am more in their minds than I have ever been before, because they have found out my secret, which has been the torture of my life. I wonder if Clemency has heard anything about it."

"I will go and see," replied James.

The minute he saw Clemency, who was in the parlor, he knew that she knew. By her side on the floor was the *Stanbridge Record*. She looked at James and pointed to it without a word. Her face was white as death. James took up the paper. That merely announced the fact of Mrs. Gordon's death, dwelt upon her many beautiful qualities of mind and body, her great suffering, and stated briefly the astonishment with which the news was received that she was Doctor Gordon's wife, and not his sister, as people had been led to suppose. "Little Annie Codman just brought it over," said Clemency. "She said her mother sent it. It is just like her mother. Mr. Codman never would have done such a thing."

Mr. Codman was the minister.

James, for a second, did not know what to say. He thought of the absurd story which he had told, or rather suggested, at the store, and realized that such a fabrication would not answer here.

Immediately Clemency fired a point-blank question at him. "Who am I?" she asked.

"You are Doctor Gordon's niece, dear."

"But—she was not my mother."

"No, dear."

"Who am I?"

"You are the daughter of Doctor Gordon's youngest sister, who died when you were born."

Clemency sat reflecting, her forehead knit, a keen look in her blue eyes. "I knew my father was dead," she said after a little. "Uncle Tom has always told me that he passed away three months before I was born, but—" She raised a puzzled, shocked, grieved face to James. "What is my name?" she asked. "My real name?"

James hesitated. Then his mind reverted to the tale which he had told at the store. He could see no other way out of the difficulty. "Did you never hear of two brothers marrying two sisters, dear?" he asked.

Clemency gazed at him with a puzzled, almost suspicious, look. "I knew I had an aunt and cousin in England named Ewing," she said, "but I always supposed that my English aunt was not my real aunt, only my aunt by marriage, that she had married my father's brother."

"Your English aunt is your uncle's own sister," said James.

"I see: my own mother and my aunt were sisters, and they married brothers," Clemency said slowly.

"That is unusual, but not unprecedented," said James. He had never been involved in such a web of fabrication. He felt his cheeks burning. He was sure that he looked guilty, but Clemency did not seem to notice it. She was reflecting, still with that puzzled knitting of her forehead and that introspective look in her blue eyes. "I wonder if I look in the least like my own mother?" she said in a curious voice, as of one who feels her way.

"Once your uncle said to me that you were your own mother's very image," replied James eagerly. He was glad to have the chance to say anything truthful.

Clemency's face lightened. She spoke with that fatuous innocence and romance of young girls, and often of older women, to whom romance and sentiment are in the place of reason. "Then I know who that man was," she announced in a delighted voice. "You and Uncle Tom thought I would never know, but I do know. I have found out my own self."

"Who was he, dear?"

"Oh, I don't know who he was really, and I don't know who that woman was. She does mix up things a good deal, but this much I do know—why Uncle Tom passed off my aunt for my mother, and why we were always hiding from that man. He was in love with my mother, and he was in love with me, because I am so much like her. Now, tell me honest, dear, didn't Uncle Tom ever tell you that that man was in love with my mother before I was born?"

"Yes, dear," James answered, fairly bewildered over the fashion in which truth was lending itself to the need of falsehood.

Clemency nodded her head triumphantly. "There, I told you I knew," said she. "Poor man, it was dreadful of him to pursue me so, and make us all so unhappy, and of course I never could have married him, even if it had not been for you. I do think he looked like a wicked man, and of course I never could have endured the thought of marrying a man who had been in love with my mother, even if he had been ever so good. But I can't help being sorry for him; he must have loved my mother so much, and he must have wasted his whole life; and then to die among strangers so suddenly, poor man."

James felt a sort of pleasure at hearing the girl express, all unknowingly, sympathy for her dead father. The tears actually stood in her eyes. "The queerest thing to me is that woman," she added musingly, after a minute. Then again her face lightened. "Why, I do believe she was his sister," she cried, "and that was the reason she wanted to get me, and the reason why she was so dreadfully upset when she heard he was dead, poor thing. Well, of course, I can't help feeling glad that I am not in danger any more; but I am sorry for that poor man, even if he wasn't good." A tear rolled visibly down Clemency's cheeks. Then she got out her handkerchief and sobbed violently. "Oh, I haven't realized," she moaned, "I haven't realized until this minute, how terrible it is that she wasn't my mother."

"She was as good as a mother to you, dear."

"Yes, I know, but she wasn't, and it hurts me worse now she is gone than it would have done when she was alive. I don't seem to have anything."

"You have me."

Then Clemency ran to him, and he held her on his knee and comforted her, then tore himself away to make his morning round of calls. Clemency followed him to the door, and kissed her hand to him as he drove away. James had good reason to remember it, for it was the last loving salutation from her for many a day.

When he returned at noon the girl's manner was unaccountably changed toward him. She only spoke to him directly when addressed, and then in monosyllables. She never looked at him. She sat at the table at luncheon and poured the chocolate, and there was almost absolute silence. Emma waited jerkily as usual. James fancied once, when he met her eyes, that there was an expression of covert triumph on her face. Emma had never liked him. He had been conscious of the fact, but it had not disturbed him. He had no more thought of this middle-aged, harsh-featured New Jersey farmer's daughter than he had of one of the dining-chairs. Gordon sat humped upon himself, as he sat nowadays, a marked stoop of age was becoming visible in his broad shoulders, and he ate perfunctorily without a word. James, after a number of futile attempts to talk to Clemency, subsided himself into bewildered silence, and ate with very little appetite. There were chops and potatoes and peas, and apple-pie, for luncheon. When it came to the pie Emma served Clemency and Doctor Gordon, and deliberately omitted James. Nobody seemed to notice it, although James felt sure that the omission was intentional. He felt himself inwardly amused at the antagonism which could take such a form, and went without his pie uncomplainingly, while Gordon and Clemency ate theirs. The dog at this juncture came slinking into the room and close to James, who gave him a lump of sugar from the bowl which happened to stand near him. At once Emma took the bowl and moved it to another part of the table out of his reach. James felt a strong inclination to laugh.

The dog sat up and begged for more sugar, and James, when they all left the table, coolly took a handful of sugar from the bowl and carried it into the office, the dog leaping at his side. Emma slammed the dining-room door behind him. Clemency, without a look at him, immediately ran upstairs to her own room. Gordon and James sat down in the office as usual for a smoke until James should start upon his afternoon rounds. Gordon asked him a few questions about the patients whom he had seen that morning, but in a listless, abstracted fashion, then he spoke of those whom James would see that afternoon. "You had better take the team," he said.

"Clemency is going with me," James said.

Gordon looked at him with faint surprise. "I think you must be mistaken," he said. "Clemency came to me just before luncheon and asked if I had any objections to her spending a few days with Annie Lipton. I told her we could get on perfectly well without her, and Aaron is going to drive her over. She will have to take a suitcase. I knew you had to go in another direction, and could not take her. I thought the change would do her good. Didn't she say anything to you about it?"

"I think it will do her good. She needs a little change," James replied evasively. As he spoke Aaron came out of the stable leading the bay mare harnessed to a buggy.

"She is going right away," said Gordon, looking a little puzzled.

He had hardly finished speaking before Clemency's voice was heard in the hall. It rang rather hard, but quite clearly. "Good-by," she called out.

"Good-by," responded Gordon and James together. Gordon looked at James, astonished that he did not go out to assist Clemency into the buggy, and bid her good-by. He seemed about to question him, then he took another puff at his pipe, and his face settled into its wonted expression of gloomy retrospection. Boy's and girl's love affairs seemed as motes in a beam of sunlight to him at this juncture.

James started to go, the horses were stamping uneasily in the drive, and he had a long round of calls to make that afternoon.

Gordon removed his pipe. "I am putting a good deal on you, Elliot," he said with a kind of hard sadness.

"That's all right," James replied cheerfully, "I am strong. I can stand it if the patients can. I fancied old Mrs. Steen was rather disgusted to see me this morning. I heard her say something about sendin' a boy to her daughter, and when I went into the bedroom, she glared at me, and said, 'You?'" James laughed.

"Her case is not at all desperate," Gordon said gloomily. "She is merely on the downward road of life. Nothing ails her except that. You can supply the few inadequate crutches of tonics as well as any one. There is not one desperately sick patient on the whole list now, that I know of, although I must confess that that Willoughby girl rather puzzles me. She breaks every diagnosis all to pieces."

"Hysteria," said James.

"Oh, yes, I know hysteria is a good way to account for our own lack of insight," said Gordon, "and it may be that girls are queer subjects. Sometimes I wonder if they know what they know. Lilian Willoughby does not."

Gordon, to James's intense surprise, flared into a burst of anger. "Yes, she does know," he declared. "Down in her inner consciousness I believe she does, poor little overstrung, oversensitive girl, half-fed, as to her body, on coarse food which she cannot assimilate, starved emotionally. If a girl like that has to exist anyway, why cannot she be born under different circumstances? That girl as daughter of a New Jersey farmer is an anomaly. If she mates at all it must be with another New Jersey farmer, then she dies after bringing a few degenerates into the world. Providence does things like that, and the doctors are supposed to right things.

That girl has had symptoms of about every known disease, and my diagnosis has failed to prove the existence of one of them. Yet there are the symptoms. Call it hysteria, or what you will. I call it an injustice on the part of the Higher Power. I suppose that is blasphemy, but I am forced to it. Can that girl help the longings for her rights, her longings which are abnormally acute because of her over-fine nervous system? Those longings, situated as she is, can never be satisfied in any way except for her own harm. Meantime she eats her own heart, since she has nothing else, and heart-eating produces all kinds of symptoms. I am absolutely powerless in such a case, though sometimes I make a diagnosis which I think may be correct, sometimes I think there is some organic trouble which I can mitigate. But always I fall back upon the miserable truth which I am convinced underlies her whole existence. She is a creature born into a life which does not and never will afford her the proper food for her physical and spiritual needs. Oh, the horror in this world, and what am I to set myself to right it? Shut the door."

"The horses are uneasy," James said.

"Never mind, shut the door. Clemency is away, and Emma out in the kitchen. I must speak to somebody, or I shall go mad."

James shut the door and turned to Gordon, who sat rigid in his chair, his hands clutching the arms. "Do you think I did right?" he groaned. "You know what I did. Was it right?"

"If you mean about your wife," James said, "I think you did entirely right."

"But you could not," Gordon returned bitterly. "It was too much for you to attempt, and yet she was nothing to you as she was to me, and the sin would not have been so terrible."

"I had not the courage," James replied simply.

"You did not think it right. You did not wish to burden your soul with such a responsibility. I was wrong to try to shift it upon you, wrong and cowardly, but she was bone of my bone and flesh of my flesh; it was a double crime for me, murder and suicide. It was not because you had not the courage: you have faced surgical operations and dissecting. You dared not commit what you were not sure was not a crime. There is no use in your hedging, Elliot. I know the truth."

"Still I think you did right," James said stubbornly. "She had to die anyway. Death was upon her. You simply hastened it."

Gordon looked at James, and his eyes seemed to fairly blaze

with somber fire; for a moment the young man thought his reason was unhinged. "But what am I? Who is any man to take whip or spur to the decrees of the Almighty, to hasten them?"

"She was suffering—" James began.

"What of that? Who can say, though she had led the life of a saint on earth, so far as any one could see, what subtle sins of life itself her pains were counteracting? Who can tell but I have deprived her of untold joys which would have compensated a thousand times for those pains by shortening them?"

"Doctor Gordon, you are morbid," James said, looking at him uneasily.

"How do you know I am morbid? Then that other—Mendon. Who is to say that I was right even about that? It is probable I saved your life, and possibly my own, as well as Clemency from misery. But who can say that death would not have been better for both you and me than life, and even misery for Clemency had that man lived? God had allowed him life upon the earth. I may have shortened that life. He was a monster of wickedness, but who can say that he was not a weapon of God, and that I have not done incalculable mischief by depriving him of that weapon? There is only one consolation which I have with regard to him; unless my diagnosis was entirely at fault, he would have had that attack of erysipelas anyway. I hardly think I deceive myself with regard to that, and there is a very probable chance that the attack would have been fatal. He had nearly lost his life twice before with the same disease. That I know, and I do not think that unless the poison was already in his blood, it would have developed so rapidly from that slight bruise. So far as the simple wound from the dog went, he was in no danger whatever. I have that consolation in his case, in not being absolutely certain that I caused his death; I am not even absolutely sure that I hastened it by any appreciable time. He might have been attacked that very night with the disease. Still there is, and always will be, the slight doubt."

"I don't think you ought to brood over that, Doctor Gordon," James said soothingly. He went close to the older man and laid a hand upon his shoulder. Gordon looked up at him, and his face was convulsed. He spoke with solemn and tragic emphasis. "It is not for mortal man to interfere with the ways of God, and he does so at his own peril," he said.

CHAPTER XIV

The confidence which Gordon had reposed in James seemed for a time to have given him a measure of relief. While he never for an instant appeared like his old self, while the games of euchre at Georgie K.'s were not resumed, nor the boyish enjoyment of things, which James now recognized to have been simply feverish attempts to live through the horrible ordeal of his life and keep his sanity, while he had now settled down into a state of austere gloom, yet he begun again to attend to his practice and to take interest in it. Clemency remained away for a week. Then Gordon brought her home. She was at the dinner-table that night when James returned rather late from a call on a far-off patient. She simply said, "Good evening! Doctor Elliot," as if he had been the merest acquaintance, and went on to serve his soup. James gave her a bewildered, half-grieved, half-angered look, which she seemed not to notice. Immediately after dinner she went to her own room. James, smoking with Gordon in the office, heard her go upstairs. Gordon nodded at James through the cloud of smoke.

"She has taken a notion, my son," he said. "She told me on the way home that she wished to break the engagement with you. She would give no reason. She wished me to tell you. I don't take her seriously. She cares as much for you as ever. Girls are queer cattle. She has some utterly unimaginable idea in her head, which will run itself out. If I were you I would pay no attention to it. Simply take her at her word, and let her alone for a little while, and she herself will urge you for a reconciliation. I know the child. She simply cannot remain at odds for any length of time with any one whom she loves, and she does love you; but she is freakish, and at times inclined to strain at her bit. Perhaps Annie Lipton has been putting ideas into her head against marriage in general. She may have frightened her, and they may have sworn celibacy together in the watches of the night. Girls hatch more mischief when they ought to be asleep. They are queer cattle."

"The trouble began before Clemency went away," James said soberly. He was quite pale.

"Trouble? What trouble?"

"I don't know. All I know is, that the very day when Clemency went away she seemed changed to me. You remember how she called out good-by, and I did not go out to help her off as I should naturally have done."

"Yes, I do remember that, and I did wonder at your not going."

"I did not go because I was quite sure that she did not wish it. She had been very curt with me, and had shown me unmistakably that my attentions were not welcome."

"And you don't know why? There had been no quarrel?"

"Not the slightest. I have not the faintest idea what the trouble is or was, and why she wishes to break the engagement. All I know is that as suddenly as a weather vane turns from west to north, she turned, and seemed to have no more use for me."

"Queer," Gordon said reflectively. He eyed James keenly. "You absolutely know of no reason?"

"I absolutely know of none. Clemency is the very first girl about whom I have ever thought in this way. There is nothing in my whole life, past or present, which I could not spread before her like an open book, so far as any fear lest it should turn her against me."

"I questioned her," Gordon said, "and she absolutely refused to give me any reason for breaking her engagement. She simply repeated over and over, 'I have changed my mind, Uncle Tom.' I asked her if she had seen anybody else."

James flushed hotly. "What did she say to that?"

"She said, 'Whom could I have seen, Uncle Tom? You yourself know how many men I have seen here, and you know I never see men at Annie's.' There is no one else. You may be sure of that, and also sure that she still cares for you. I know that from her whole manner. She has simply taken one of those unaccountable freaks which the best of girls will take. Just let her alone, and the whole will right itself. She may have got a sudden scare at the idea of marriage itself, for all I know. I still cling to the idea that Annie Lipton has been putting ideas into her head, in spite of what you say of her coldness before she went there. She may have started herself in the path, but Annie helped her further on."

"Of course I must leave here," James said gloomily.

Gordon started. "Leave here?"

"Yes, of course. Clemency will naturally not wish to have me a member of the household in the existing state of things."

"Clemency will wish it. Of course you are going to stay, Elliot."

"I don't feel as if I could, Doctor Gordon."

"Nonsense!"

"It will naturally not be very pleasant for me," James said, coloring.

"Why not?" asked Gordon irritably. "You are not a love-sick girl."

"No, I am not," James returned with spirit. "I know I am jilted, but I mean to take, and I think I am taking it, like a man. If Clemency does not want me, I am sure I do not want her to have me. And I can stand seeing her daily under the altered condition of things. I am no milk-sop. Generally speaking, living under a roof when you are an object of aversion to a member of the household, is not exactly pleasant."

"You are not an object of aversion."

"I might as well be."

Gordon looked at the young man pitifully. "For God's sake, then don't leave *me*, Elliot," he said.

James stared at him. There was so much emotion in his face.

"What do you think my life would be without you?" said Gordon. "Aside from your assistance, which I cannot do without, you are my only solace, especially since Clemency is in this mood. Stay for my sake, if it is unpleasant, Elliot."

"Well, I will stay, if you feel so about it, doctor," James replied.

"Clemency is treating you shamefully," Gordon said.

"A girl has a right to her own mind in such a matter, if she has in anything."

"The worst of it is, it is not her mind. I tell you I know that."

"I am not so sure."

"Wait and see! You underestimate yourself, boy."

James laughed sadly. Then there was a knock on the office door and Georgie K. appeared. He looked shyly at Gordon. He had a bottle under his arm. "I have brought over a little apple-jack; thought it might do you good," he stammered, his great face suffused like a girl's.

Gordon looked affectionately at him. "Thank you, Georgie K.," he said. "Sit down and we will have a game. I'll get the hot water and glasses. Emma is out."

"I'll get them," James said eagerly. He went out to the kitchen, but Emma was not out. She was sitting sewing in a gingham apron.

"What do you want?" she demanded severely.

James explained meekly.

"Well, go back to the office, and I'll fetch the things," Emma said in a hostile tone. James obeyed. Presently Emma appeared bearing a tray with the hot water and two glasses, Gordon did not notice the omission of a third glass, until she had gone out. "Why, she only brought two glasses," he said.

James felt absurdly unequal to facing Emma again. "I don't think I'll take anything tonight," he said.

"Nonsense!" returned Gordon. He went to the door and shouted for Emma with no response. "She can't have gone upstairs so quickly," he said. But when after another shout he got no response, he went himself into the dining-room, and got a tumbler from the sideboard. "She must have gone upstairs at once," he remarked when he returned. "The kitchen is dark."

Georgie K. did not remain very late. He seemed nervously solicitous with regard to Doctor Gordon. When he left he shook hands with him, and bade him take good care of himself.

"I love that man," Gordon said, when the door had closed behind him.

When James entered his room that night he found fresh proof of Emma's inexplicable hostility. The room was in total darkness. He lit matches and searched for lamp or candles, to find none. He fumbled his way out into the kitchen, and got a little lamp, which gave but a dim light, and read, as was his habit, after he had gone to bed, with exceeding difficulty. He also was subjected to a most absurd annoyance from the presence of some gritty particles in the bed. After he extinguished his lamp he could not go to sleep because of them, and lit his lamp again, and tore the sheet off and shook it. The gritty particles seemed to him to be crumbs of very hard and dry bread. He made the bed up again after his clumsy masculine fashion. James had not much manual dexterity, and rested very uncomfortably, from a pronounced inclination of the coverings to slide off his feet, and over one side of the bed.

The next morning Emma did not bring hot water for his shaving. She usually set a pitcher outside his door, but this morning there was none. He was obliged to go out to the kitchen and prefer a request for some. "I have jest filled up the coffee-pot and the tea-kettle, and I guess the water ain't very hot," Emma said in a malicious tone, as she filled a pitcher for him.

The water was not very hot. James had a severe experience shaving, and his annoyances were not over then. There was no napkin beside his plate at breakfast. He did not like to apply to Clemency, whose cold good morning had served to establish a higher barrier between them, and who sat behind the coffee urn with a forlorn but none the less severe look. He also did not like to apply to Gordon for fear of offending her. It was about as bad to ask Emma, but he finally did, in a low tone.

Emma apparently did not hear. He was forced to repeat his request for a napkin loudly. Gordon looked up. "Emma, why do you not set the table properly?" he asked, in a severe tone.

Emma tossed her head and muttered. She brought a napkin, and laid it beside James's plate with an impetus as if it had been a lump of lead. Presently James discovered that he had only one spoon, but he made that do duty for his cereal and coffee, and said nothing. He was aware of Emma's eyes of covert, malicious enjoyment upon him, as he surreptitiously licked off the oatmeal, and put the spoon in his coffee. He began to wonder what he could do, if this state of things was to continue. It all seemed so absurd, the grievances were so exceedingly petty. He could not imagine what had so turned Emma against him. He was even more at a loss where she was concerned than in Clemency's case. A girl engaged might find some foolish reason, which seemed enormous to her, to turn the cold shoulder to him, but it was inconceivable that Emma should. He had always treated her politely, even with a certain deference, knowing, as he did, that she was an old and faithful servant, and as the daughter of a farmer being, in her own estimation at least, of a highly superior station to that of servants in general. He could not imagine why Emma was subjecting him to these ridiculous persecutions, before which he was almost helpless. She had heretofore treated him loftily, as was her wont with everybody, except Gordon and Clemency, but certainly she had neglected none of her duties with regard to him. Miserable as James was concerning Clemency, he could not but feel that if he were to be subjected to these incomprehensible annoyances from Emma, life in the house would be almost impossible. He could bear sorrow like a man, but to bear pinpricks beside was almost too much to ask. That noon, when he returned from his rounds, he realized that there was to be no cessation. Clemency was not at the lunch-table. Gordon said she had a headache and was lying down. Emma in passing James his cup of tea, contrived to spill it over him. He was not scalded, but his shirt-front and collar were stained, thereby necessitating a change, and he was in a hurry to be gone directly after lunch.

Gordon roused himself, however. "Be more careful another time, Emma," he said sharply.

Emma tossed her head. "Doctor Elliot moved jest as I was coming with the cup," she said in a thin, waspish voice.

"He did no such thing," Gordon said harshly, "and if he had, it was your business to be careful. Get Doctor Elliot another cup of tea."

Emma obeyed with a jerk. She set the cup and saucer down beside James's plate as hard as she dared, and James at the first sip found that the tea was salted. However, he said nothing. Gordon after his outburst had resumed his former state of apathy, and was eating and drinking like a machine, whose works were rusty and almost run down. He could not trouble him with such an absurdity. Then, too, he was too vexed to please the girl so much. He forced himself to drink the tea without a grimace, knowing that Emma's eyes were upon him. But the climax was almost reached. That night when on his return he wished to change his collar before dinner, he found every one with the buttonholes torn. It was skilfully done, so skilfully that no one could have declared positively that it had not been done accidentally in the laundry. James would not appear at the dinner-table in a soiled collar, and was forced to hurry out to the village store and purchase new ones. These, with the exception of the one he put on, he locked in his trunk. He was late for dinner, and the soup was quite cold. When Doctor Gordon complained irritably, Emma replied with one of her characteristic tosses of the head that she couldn't help it, Doctor Elliot was late. James said nothing. He swallowed his lukewarm soup in silence. He began to wonder what he could do. He did not wish to complain to Doctor Gordon, especially as the result might be the dismissal of Emma, and he felt that he could say nothing to Clemency about it. Clemency appeared at the dinner-table, but she looked pale and forlorn, and said good evening to James without lifting her eyes. When her uncle asked if her head was better, she said, "Yes, thank you," in a spiritless tone. She ate almost nothing. After dinner, James had a call to make, and, on his return, entered by the office door. He found Gordon fast asleep in his chair, with the dog at his feet. The dog started up at sight of James, but he motioned him down, and went softly out into the hall. There was a light there, but none in the parlor. James heard distinctly a little sob from the parlor. He hesitated a moment, then he entered the room. It was suffused with moonlight. All the pale objects stood out like ghosts. Clemency by the window, in a little white wool house-gown, looked, ghostly.

James went straight across to her, pulled up a chair beside her, seated himself, and pulled one of her little hands away from her face almost roughly, and held it firmly in spite of her weak attempt to remove it. "Now, Clemency," he said in a determined voice, "this has gone quite far enough. You told your uncle that you wished to break your engagement to me. I have no wish to coerce you. If you really do not want to marry me, why, I must make the best of it, but I have a right to know the reason why, and I will know it."

Clemency was silent, except for her sobs.

"Tell me," said James.

"Don't," whispered Clemency.

"Tell me."

Then Clemency let her other hand, which contained a moist little ball of handkerchief, fall. She turned full upon him her tearful, swollen face. "If you want to know what you know already," said she, in a hard voice, "here it is. She wasn't my mother, but I loved her like one, and you killed her."

CHAPTER XV

James sat as if turned to stone. All in a second he realized what it must be. He let Clemency's hand go, and leaned back in his chair. "What do you mean, Clemency?" he asked finally, but he realized how senseless the question was. He knew perfectly well what she meant, and he knew perfectly well that he was utterly helpless before her accusation.

"You know," said Clemency, still in her unnatural hard voice. "You killed her."

"How?"

"You know. You gave her more morphine, and her heart was weak. Emma overheard Uncle Tom say so, and that more morphine was dangerous. She might have been alive today if it had not been for you."

James sat staring at the girl. She went on pitilessly. "You did not see Emma that last time you came upstairs," she said, "but she saw you. She was standing in the door of her room, and she had no light. She saw you and Mrs. Blair going away from her room, and she heard Mrs. Blair tell you she was dead. You killed her. I want nothing whatever to do with a murderer."

James remembered that draught of cold air. It must have come from the open door of Emma's room at the end of the hall. He understood that Emma could not have seen him coming upstairs, but that she had seen him with Mrs. Blair at the door of the sick-room, and had jumped at her conclusion.

"Emma knew when you went upstairs first," said Clemency. "You left her door a little ajar. Emma saw you giving her a hypodermic. And then when that did not kill her you gave her another. Uncle Tom did not know. He must never know, for it would kill him, but you did kill her."

James was silent for a moment. He realized the impossibility of clearing himself from the accusation unless he told the whole truth and implicated Doctor Gordon. Finally he said, miserably enough, "You don't know how horribly she was suffering, dear. You don't know what torments she would have had to suffer."

He knew when he said that that he incriminated himself. Clemency retorted immediately, "You don't know. I have heard Uncle Tom say that nobody can ever know. She might have gotten well. Anyway, you killed her." With that Clemency sprang up and ran out of the room, and James heard her sob.

As for himself, he remained where he was for a long time. He never knew how long. He felt numb. He realized himself to be in a gulf of misunderstanding, from which he could not be extricated, even for the sake of Clemency. It seemed to him again that he must go away, but he remembered Gordon's pitiful plea to him to remain. Finally he went into his room, to find that Emma, in her absurd malice, had left only the coverlid on the bed. She had stripped it of the sheets and blankets. He lay down with his clothes on and passed a sleepless night.

The next morning at the breakfast-table he looked haggard and pale. He could eat nothing. Doctor Gordon looked at him keenly.

"What is the matter, Elliot?" he asked.

Clemency gave a quick glance at him, and her face worked.

"Nothing," replied James.

"You look downright ill."

"I am not ill."

Clemency rose abruptly and left the table.

"What is the matter, Clemency? Where are you going?" Gordon called out.

"I have finished my breakfast," the girl replied in a stifled voice.

Gordon insisted on making some calls that morning, and relieving James. "You are worn out, my son," he said in a voice of real affection, and clapped him on the shoulder. He sent James on a short round in spite of his objections, and the consequence was that James reached home half an hour before luncheon.

It was a beautiful morning. Spring seemed to have come with a winged leap. A faint down of green shaded the elms, and there was a pink cloud of peach bloom in the distance. The cherry trees were swollen almost to blossom, and the apple trees had pale radiances in the glance of the sun. The grass was quite green, and here and there were dandelions. Clemency was out in the yard, working in a little flower-garden, as James drove in. She had on a black dress, and her fair head was uncovered. She pretended not to see James, but he had hardly entered the office before she came in. Her face was all suffused with pink. She looked at him tenderly and angrily.

"Are you ill?" she said, in an indignant voice which had, in spite of herself, soft cadences.

"No, Clemency."

"Then why do you look so?" she demanded.

James turned at that. "Clemency, you accuse me of cruelty," he said, "but you yourself are cruel. You do not realize that you cannot tell a man he is a murderer, and throw him over when he loves you, and yet have him utterly unmoved by it."

Suddenly Clemency was in his arms. "I love you, I love you," she sobbed. "Don't be unhappy, don't look so. It breaks my heart. I love you, I do love you, dear. I can't marry you, but I love you!"

"If you love me, you can marry me."

Clemency shrank away, then she clung to him again. "No," she said, "I can't get over the thought of it. I can't help it, but I do love you. We will go on just the same as ever, only we will not get married. You know we were not going to get married just yet anyway. I love you. We will go on just the same. Only don't look the way you did this morning at breakfast."

"How did I look?"

"As if your heart were broken."

"So it is, dear."

"No, it is not. I love you, I tell you. What is the need of bothering about marriage anyway? I am perfectly happy being engaged. Annie says she is never going to get married. Let the marriage alone. Only you won't look so any more, will you, dear?"

CHAPTER XVI

After this James encountered a strange state of things: the semblance of happiness, which almost deceived him as to its reality.

Clemency was as loving as she had ever been. Gordon congratulated James upon the reconciliation. "I knew the child could never hold out, and it was Annie Lipton," he said. James admitted that Annie Lipton might have been the straw which turned the balance. He knew that Clemency had not told Gordon of her conviction that he had given the final dose of morphine to her aunt. Everything now went on as before. Clemency suddenly became awake to Emma's petty persecutions of James, and they ceased. James one day could not help overhearing a conversation between the two. He was in the stable, and the kitchen windows were open. He heard only a few words. "You don't mean to say you are goin' to hev him?" said Emma in her strident voice.

"No, I am not," returned Clemency's sweet, decided one.

"What be you goin' with him again for then?"

James knew how the girl blushed at that, but she answered with spirit. "That is entirely my own affair, Emma," she said, "and as long as Doctor Elliot remains under this roof, and pays for it, too, he must be treated decently. You don't pass him things, you don't fill his lamp. Now you must treat him exactly as you did before, or I shall tell Uncle Tom."

"You won't tell him why?" said Emma, and there was alarm in her voice, for she adored Gordon.

"Did you ever know me to go from one to another in such a way?" asked Clemency. "You know if I told Uncle Tom, he would not put up with it a minute. He thinks the world of Doctor Elliot."

"It's awful queer how men folks can be imposed on," said Emma.

"That has nothing to do with it," Clemency said. "You must treat Doctor Elliot respectfully, Emma."

"I'm jest as good as he be," said Emma resentfully.

"Well, what if you are? He's as good as you, isn't he? And he treats you civilly. He always has."

"I'm a good deal better than he be," Emma went on irascibly. "I wouldn't have gone and went, and—"

"Hush!" ordered Clemency in a frightened voice. "Emma, you must do as I say."

James drove out of the yard and heard no more, but after that he had no fault to find with Emma, so far as her service was concerned. It is true that she gave him malignant glances, but she made him comfortable, albeit unwillingly. It was fortunate for him that she did so, or he would have found his position almost unbearable. Doctor Gordon relaxed again into his state of apathetic gloom. His strength also seemed to wane. Almost the whole practice devolved upon James. Gordon seemed less and less interested even in extreme cases. Georgie K. also lost his power over him. Now and then of an evening he came, but Gordon, save to offer him a cigar, took scarcely any notice of him. One evening Georgie K. made a motion to James behind Gordon's back when he took leave, and James made an excuse to follow him out. In the drive Georgie K. took James by the arm, and the young man felt him tremble. "What ails him?" asked Georgie K.

"I hardly know," James replied in a whisper.

"I know," said Georgie K. By the light from the office window James could see that the man was actually weeping. His great ruddy face was streaming with tears. "Don't I know?" he sobbed.

James remembered the stuffed canary and the wax flowers, and the story Gordon had told him of Georgie K.'s grief over his wife's death.

"I dare say you are right," he returned.

"He's breakin' his heart, that's what he's doin'," said Georgie K. "Can't you get him to go away for a change or somethin'?"

"I have tried."

"He'll die of it," Georgie K. said with a great gulp as he went out of the yard.

When James reëntered the office Gordon looked up at him. "That poor old fellow called you out to talk about me," he said quietly. "I know I'm going downhill."

"For heaven's sake, can't you go up, doctor?"

"No, I am done for. I could get over losing her, but I can't get over what—you know what."

"But her death was inevitable, and greater agony was inevitable."

Gordon turned upon him fiercely. "When you have been as long in this cursed profession as I have," he said, "you will realize that nothing is inevitable. She might have recovered for all I know. That woman, at Turner Hill, who I thought was dying six months ago, being up and around again, is an instance. I tell you mortal man has no right to thrust his hand between the Almighty and fate. You know nothing, and I know nothing."

"I do know."

"You don't know, and you don't even know that you don't know. There is no use talking about this any longer. When I am gone you must marry Clemency, and keep on with my practice."

James considered when he was in his own room that the event of his succeeding to the practice might not be so very remote, but as to his marrying Clemency he doubted. He dared not hint of the matter to Gordon, for he knew it would disturb him, but Clemency, as the days went on, became more and more variable. At times she was loving, at times it was quite evident that she shrank from him with a sort of involuntary horror. James began to wonder if they ever could marry. He was fully resolved not to clear himself at the expense of Doctor Gordon; in fact, such a course never occurred to him. He had a very simple straightforwardness in matters of honor, and this seemed to him a matter of honor. No question with regard to it arose in his mind. Obviously it was better that he should bear the brunt than Gordon, but he did ask himself if it would ever be possible for Clemency to dissociate him from the thought of the tragedy entirely, and if she could not, would it be possible for her to be happy as his wife? That very day Clemency had avoided him, and once when he had approached she had visibly shrunk and paled. Evidently the child could not help it. She looked miserably unhappy. She had grown thin lately, and had lost almost entirely her sense of fun, which had always been so ready.

James went to sleep, wondering how she would treat him the next day. He never knew, for the girl shifted like a weather-cock, driven hither and yon by her love and terror like two winds. The next day, however, solved the problem in an entirely unexpected fashion. James, that morning after breakfast, during which Clemency had sat pale and stern behind the coffee-urn, and scarcely had noticed him, set off on a round of calls. Doctor Gordon, to his surprise, announced his intention of making some calls himself; he said that he would take the team, and James must drive the balky mare, as the bay was to be taken to the blacksmith's. Gordon that morning looked worse than usual, although he evinced such unwonted energy. He trembled like a very old man. He ate scarcely anything, and his mouth was set hard with a desperate expression.

James wished to urge him to remain at home, but he did not dare. Gordon, when he left the breakfast-table, proposed that James should take Clemency with him, but the girl replied curtly that she was too busy. Gordon started on his long circuit, and James set off to make the rounds of Alton and Westover. The mare seemed in a very favorable mood that morning. She did not balk, and went at a good pace. It was not until James was on his homeward road that the trouble began. Then the mare planted her four feet at angles, in her favorite fashion, and became as immovable as a horse of bronze. James touched her with the whip. He was in no patient mood that morning. Finally he lashed her. He might as well have lashed a stone, for all the effect his blows had. Then he got out and tried coaxing. She did not seem to even see him. Her great eyes had a curious introspective expression. Then he got again into the buggy and sat still. A sense of obstinacy as great as the animal's came over him. "Stand there and be damned!" he said.

"Go without your dinner if you want to." He leaned back in a corner of the buggy, and began reflecting.

His reflections were at once angry and gloomy. He was, he told himself, tired of the situation. He began to wonder if he ought not, for the sake of self-respect, to leave Alton and Clemency. He wondered if a man ought to submit to be so treated, and yet he recognized Clemency's own view of the situation, and a great wave of love and pity for the poor child swept over him. The mare had halted in a part of the road where there were no houses, and flowering alders filled the air with their faint sweetness. Under that sweetness, like the bass in a harmony, he could smell the pines in the woods on either hand. He also heard their voices, like the waves of the sea. It was a very warm day, one of those days in which Spring makes leaps toward Summer. James felt uncomfortably heated, for the buggy was in the full glare of sunlight. All his solace came from the fact that he himself, sitting there so quietly, was outwitting the mare by showing as great obstinacy as her own. He knew that she inwardly fretted at not arousing irritation. That a tickle, even a lash of the whip, would delight her. He sat still, leaning his head back. He was almost asleep when he heard a rumble of heavy wheels, and looking ahead languidly perceived a wagon laden with household goods of some spring-flitters approaching. He sat still and watched the great wagon drawn by two lean, white horses, and piled high with the poor household belongings—miserable wooden chairs and feather beds, and a child's cradle rocking imminently on the top. A lank Jerseyman was driving. By his side on the high seat was his stout wife holding a baby. The weak wail of the child filled the air. James looked to make sure that there was room for the team to pass. He thought there was, and sat idly watching them. The woman looked at him, made some remark to the man, and then both grinned weakly, recognizing the situation. The man on the team drove carefully, but a stone on the outer side caused his team to swerve a trifle. The wheels hit the wheels of the buggy, and the cradle tilted swiftly on to the back of the balky mare, and she bolted. In all her experience of a long, balky life, a cradle as a means of breaking her spirit had not been encountered. James had not time to clutch the lines which had fallen to the floor of the buggy before he was thrown out. He felt the buggy tilting to its fall, he heard a crashing sound and a fierce kicking, and then he knew no more.

When he came to himself he was on the lounge in Doctor Gordon's office. Emma was just disappearing with a pitcher in the direction of the kitchen, and he felt something cool on his forehead. He smelled aromatic salts, and heard a piteous little voice, like the bleat of a wounded lamb, in his ears, and kisses on his cheeks, and a soft hand rubbing his own. "Oh, darling," the little voice was saying, "oh, darling, are you much hurt? Are you? Please speak to me. It is Clemency. Oh, he is dead! He is dead!" Then came wild sobs, and Emma rushed into the room, and he heard her say, "Here, put this ice on his head, quick!"

James was still so faint that he could only gasp weakly. And he could open his eyes to nothing but darkness and a marvellous spinning and whir as of shadows in a wind.

"He's comin' to," said Emma. Her voice sounded as if she felt moved. "Don't take on so, Miss Clemency," she said; "he ain't dead."

Again James felt the soft kisses and tears on his face, and again came the poor little voice, "Oh, darling, please listen, please don't do so. I will marry you. I will. I know you did just right. I read one of Uncle Tom's books this morning, and I found out what awful suffering she might have had hours longer. You did right. I will marry you. I will never think of it again. Please don't look so. Are you dreadfully hurt? Oh, when they came bringing you in I thought you were killed! There is a great bruise on your head. Does it hurt much? You do feel better, don't you? Oh, Emma, if Uncle Tom would only come. Can't you hear me, dear? I will marry you. I take it all back. I will marry you! I will marry you whenever you wish. Oh, please look at me! Please speak to me! Oh, Emma, there is Uncle Tom. I am so glad."

And then poor, little Clemency, all unstrung and frightened, sank into an unconscious little heap on the floor as Gordon entered. "What the devil?" he cried out. "I saw the buggy smashed on the road, and that mare went down the Ford Hill road like a whirlwind. What, Elliot, are you hurt, boy? Clemency, Emma, what has happened?"

All the time Gordon was talking he was examining James, who was now able to speak feebly. "The mare was frightened and threw me," he gasped. "I was stunned. I am all right now. See to Clemency!"

But Clemency was already staggering weakly to her feet.

"Oh, Uncle Tom, he isn't killed, is he?" she sobbed.

"Killed, no," said Gordon, "but he will be if you don't stop crying and making a goose of yourself, Clemency."

"We put ice on his head," sobbed Clemency. "He isn't—"

"Of course he isn't. He was only stunned. That is only a flesh wound."

"I tried to git some brandy down him, but I couldn't," said Emma.

"Give it to me," said Gordon. He poured out some brandy in a spoon, and James swallowed it. "He will be all right now," Gordon said. "You won't be such a beauty that the women will run after you for a few days, Elliot, but you're all right."

"I feel all right," James said.

"It is nothing more than a little boy with a bump on his forehead," said Gordon to Clemency. "Now, child, stop crying, and go and bathe your eyes. Emma, is luncheon ready?"

When both women had gone Gordon, who had been applying some ointment to James's forehead, said in a low voice, broken by emotion, "You are all right, Elliot, but—you did have a close call."

"I suppose I did," James said, laughing feebly.

He essayed to rise, but Gordon held him down. "No, keep still," he said. "You must not stir today. I will have your luncheon brought in. Clemency will be only too happy to wait on you, hand and foot."

"Poor little girl, I must have given her an awful fright," said James.

"Well, you are not exactly the looking object to do anything else," said Gordon laughing.

"Where is there a glass?"

"Where you won't have it. You won't be scarred. It is simply a temporary eclipse of your beauty, and Clemency will love you all the more for it. You need not worry. Talk about the vanity of women. I thought you were above it, Elliot. Now lie still. If you get up you will be giddy."

James lay still, smiling. He felt very happy, and his love for Clemency seemed like a glow of pure radiance in his heart. He lay on the office lounge all the afternoon. He fell asleep with Clemency sitting beside holding his hand. Gordon had gone out to finish the calls. It was six o'clock before he drove into the yard. James had just awakened and lay feeling a great peace and content. Clemency was smiling down at his discolored face, as if it were the face of an angel. The windows were open, and the distant lowing of cattle, waiting at homeward bars, the monotone of frogs, and the songs of circling swallows came in. James felt as if he saw in a celestial vision the whole world and life, and that it was all blessed and good, that even the pain and sorrow blossomed in the end into ineffable flowers of pure delight.

But when Doctor Gordon entered this vision was clouded, for Gordon's face had reassumed its old expression of settled melancholy and despair. He inquired how James found himself with an apathetic air, and then sat down and mechanically filled his pipe. After it was filled he seemed to forget to light it, so deep was his painful reverie. He sat with it in hand, staring straight ahead. Then a strange thing happened. The office door opened and Mrs. Blair, the nurse, entered. She was dressed in black, she carried a black travelling bag, and she wore a black bonnet, with a high black tuft on the top by way of trimming. Mrs. Blair was very tall, and this black tuft, when she entered the door, barely grazed the lintel.

Gordon rose and said good evening, and regarded her in a bewildered fashion, as did James and Clemency.

Mrs. Blair spoke with no preface. "I am going to leave Alton," she said in her severe voice, "and I want to tell you something first, and to say good-by." She looked at Gordon, then at the others, one after another, then at Gordon again. "I did not think at first that it would be necessary for me to say what I am going to," she continued, "but I overheard some things that were said that night, and I have been thinking—and then I heard the other day (I don't know how true it is) that Clemency and Doctor Elliot had had a falling out, and I didn't know but—I didn't quite know what anybody thought, and I wanted you all to know the truth. I didn't want any mistakes made to cause unhappiness." She hesitated, her eyes upon Doctor Gordon grew more intense. "Maybe *you* think you gave her that dose of morphine that killed her," she said steadily, "but you didn't. Doctor Elliot gave her water, and you gave her mostly water. I had diluted the morphine, and you didn't know it. I had made up my mind that she was going to have the morphine, but I had made up my mind that nobody but me should have the responsibility of it. I'm all alone in the world, and my conscience upheld me, and I felt I'd rather take the blame, if there was to be any. I made up my mind to wait till a certain time and then give it to her, and I did. I am the one who gave her the morphine that killed her. I am going to leave Alton for good. My trunk is down at the station. I came to tell you that I gave her the morphine, and if I did wrong in helping God to shorten her sufferings, I am the one to be punished, and I stand ready to bear the punishment."

Gordon looked at her. He did not speak, but it was with his face as if a mask of dreadful misery had dropped from it.

"Good-by!" said Mrs. Blair. She went out of the door, and the black tuft on her bonnet barely grazed the lintel.

THE END

www.ingramcontent.com/pod-product-compliance
Lightning Source LLC
Chambersburg PA
CBHW030515260626
47157CB00005B/1756